Space Race

Space Race

Sylvia Waugh

Delacorte Press

Published by
Delacorte Press
an imprint of
Random House Children's Books
a division of Random House, Inc.
1540 Broadway
New York, New York 10036

First American Edition 2000
First published in Great Britain by the Bodley Head Children's Books,
an imprint of the Random House Group, Ltd. 2000

Visit us on the Web! www.randomhouse.com/kids
Educators and librarians, for a variety of teaching tools, visit us at
www.randomhouse.com/teachers

Library of Congress Cataloging-in-Publication Data

Waugh, Sylvia.
   Space race / Sylvia Waugh.—1st American ed.
      p.   cm.
   Summary: When he learns that he and his father must soon leave Earth,
eleven-year-old Thomas Derwent is upset, but a terrible accident that
separates the two of them makes Thomas's situation much worse.
   ISBN 0-385-37266-8
   [1. Extraterrestrial beings—Fiction.   2. Fathers and sons—Fiction.
3. England—Fiction.   4. Science Fiction.]   I. Title.
PZ7.W35115 Sp 2000
[Fic]—dc21   99-055399

The text of this book is set in 12-point New Baskerville.

Book design by Patrice Sheridan

Manufactured in the United States of America

August 2000

10 9 8 7 6 5 4 3 2

BVG

For three of my keenest readers:
my daughter-in-law, Kathryn Waugh, née Hamill,
my cousin, Patricia Charlton,
and my friend, Elizabeth Victor

Contents

Awake! for Morning in the Bowl of Night
   Has flung the Stone that puts the Stars to flight:
   And Lo! the Hunter of the East has caught
The Sultan's Turret in a Noose of Light.

The Rubáiyát of Omar Khayyám
translated by Edward Fitzgerald

Chapter 1

The Fight

The village of Belthorp lay sleeping like the little town of Bethlehem under the dark December sky. In the streets, not a soul was stirring. The inn sign creaked as it swayed in a light breeze. A solitary cat stepped delicately along the stone wall in front of the Merrivale cottages. There were no watchers in the night, unless the twinkling stars were all gazing down on this little bit of England.

Then, suddenly, the peace was shattered.

A fire engine sped into the village from the south, hurtled along the main street, and shot out up the hillside to the north. Its siren, hee-hawing through the silent night, woke up most of the villagers. And some of them were none too pleased!

"Three o'clock in the ruddy morning!" growled Sam Swanson, the newsagent, thinking of his own early start. "What a time to be making all that racket! Who do they think's goin' to get in their way? I've a mind to report them. I'm sure it's against the rules. And if it's not, it dang well should be!''

His sons, Philip and Anthony, were hanging out of their bedroom window in the flat above the shop, eager to see whatever could be seen. Their mother came in and chased them back to bed after slamming down the window to shut out the freezing cold.

Philip yawned but grumbled, "I bet Donnie's up watching. I bet his mam isn't sending him back to bed."

"Well, *your* mam is," said Mrs. Swanson. "I don't want to hear another sound from this room."

Thomas Derwent must have been the only child in the village who slept through it all, though the engine passed right in front of his house, just below his window. Thomas had a time for sleeping and a time for waking, and nothing ever stood in the way of that routine. He had never been taught to wake up in the middle of the night. It had not been part of his training. By day he must observe. By night he was to sleep, as children do.

Next day all of the village children, except Thomas, were tired at breakfast, but not too tired to perk up and gossip on their way to school. The fire of the night before was their only topic. Jackson's barn, the oldest for miles around, with a roof that had lasted three hundred years and housed many generations of owls and owlets, had gone up in flames.

"I saw it all," said Donald Justice triumphantly. "I

put me coat on over me pajamas and made me dad take me up to see it on his motorbike. He didn't want to go at first, but I can talk him into *anything*. An' it was better than Bonfire Night. There was flames and smoke everywhere. An' we saw two owls flying out through the smoke."

Philip Swanson looked at his friend sourly.

"You'll be saying next that you're *glad* it happened. You'll be saying next you done it."

But Donnie wasn't prepared to go as far as that. Young as he was, he had the sense to realize that what had happened was awful. His freckled face reddened to the roots of his pale ginger hair.

"Don't you dare say I'd do anything like that, Phil Swanson," he said. "Just don't you dare!"

He glared at Philip and raised a threatening fist.

"Yah!" said Philip. "Yah! Yah! Di yah! Yah!" while he thought of something nastier to say.

By the time they reached the school gates, the quarrel was ready to turn to fisticuffs. They stood in the gateway facing each other. A crowd quickly gathered round.

Thomas Derwent watched them all and wondered how it had started and what would happen next. He still didn't know what Donnie was supposed to have done. It was important to find out. Then he heard a shocked little girl on the outside of the crowd saying to her friend, "Donnie done the barn fire last night!"

"If *you* didn't do it, Donnie," said Philip, poking a finger into his friend's shoulder, "then I bet it was your dad. It was sparks from that old motorbike of his."

3

"Right!" roared Donnie. "That's done it! You'll get what you're asking for."

He lunged toward Philip, fists clenched and flying.

But the fight got no further than that. Beside the gate was an iron manhole settled unevenly in the ground. It had always been there, but Donnie, in his temper, forgot to notice it. One toe stubbed against the rim. The boy lost his balance and went crashing forward, stretching out his hands to save himself.

He fell full length. His nose started to bleed and his palms filled with grit. Then he began to cry, loudly and savagely, with pain and anger.

At that moment Miss Kershaw came round the corner riding her bicycle. She heard the cries, stopped with a sigh, and thought ruefully, *Thus beginneth another bright day!*

"Come along, Donnie," she said after she'd got the boy to his feet and checked his injuries. "You're not dead yet, not by a long chalk. We'll soon get you put to rights."

She turned to the group standing there, selected Nigel, a trustworthy boy from the top class, and said, "Here, Nigel, take my bike round to the shed and padlock it. And you, Philip, had better come with Donnie and me. He'll be happier if you're with him."

The teacher led them both away to the main entrance, sacred to teachers and special dispensations.

The other children dispersed by twos and threes, girls toward one side door, boys to the other.

Only Thomas Derwent lingered by the gate. He was waiting for his own best friend to arrive. Thomas was bewildered. What was true and what was lies? How could friends be so nasty to each other? Observing was all very well, but understanding was often much too difficult. Five years of watching and listening, growing older and wiser, still left areas beyond his grasp. People are so very peculiar.

I'll have to ask Mickey, he thought. *This is a bit I should really try to understand before I write it down.*

Chapter 2

At Home at Number 13 Merrivale

"How did the day go?" said Patrick Derwent. He sat back in his armchair, ready to read the evening paper. Outside, it was a crisp and chilly winter's evening. Inside, the fire glowed in the hearth and all was snug.

His son, to whom this question was addressed, was sitting at the table by the window, an exercise book open in front of him, light from the Anglepoise lamp shining down onto the page. Thomas was chewing the end of his pen, thinking what he should write next. He looked across at his father impatiently.

"I'm writing it all down," he said. "It wasn't much different from any other day. Only Donald Justice fell down and made his nose bleed. Miss Kershaw mopped it up for him and got him to stop crying. And before that there was nearly a fight. And the boys woke up in the middle of the night when they heard the fire engine."

"But you," said Patrick very deliberately, "how did

the day go for *you*? You may not realize this, but I have often thought it was unfair to make you see life as one long report. You've been so good about it, even from being a six-year-old, struggling to tell everything in a six-year-old's words. In all our time here, never a day missed, never a grumble. I'm proud of you."

Thomas looked at his father curiously. It seemed such an odd way to talk after all this time. Thomas was eleven years old and he and his father had lived together, just the two of them, in this comfy cottage for five years now. To be honest, Thomas could hardly remember the Other Place. He had been Thomas Derwent for such a long time. The face he saw in the mirror was a familiar one—straight, fine black hair; small, bright dark eyes; a mouth for smiling and a chin already firm. In stature, he was slight enough to be bullied, but nobody ever bullied him.

"I don't mind writing it all down," he said, gesturing with his slim hand toward the book in front of him. "I've always done it, haven't I? Mostly I quite like doing it. Though I still don't know what it's for. In a way I suppose I can guess, but it doesn't seem important enough."

Patrick smiled at his son.

"You don't need to know," he said, "but do believe me, what you are doing is *very* important. Think of it as part of an enormous jigsaw, your own special contribution. It is what you are here for. I'm just sorry you had to miss your childhood years in Ormingat. Someday I'll make it up to you."

He did not say "when we go home," but his words

7

kindled in Thomas an uneasy suspicion that that was what he meant. The Other Place might be home to Patrick, but Belthorp was the only home that Thomas knew—or wanted to know, if it came to that.

Now all of that was to change. He knew nothing for sure, but his father's words sounded a warning.

His suspicions made it hard to concentrate. The pen on the page struggled to tell the story of the day, that particular day, in every detail, including the playground fight, the mental arithmetic lesson, the mystery spelling test, and the fact that Mickey Trent was off "bad"—crossed out—no, "ill."

Patrick turned the pages in the local paper regretfully. For him, leaving Belthorp should have been just another move, but he too had become used to the place and the people, settled there, willing to take root. It was something he had been warned about at the very start. But warnings don't confer immunity. Patrick read details of the Christmas bazaar to be held in the village hall, then the story of a dog lost down a pothole . . . and he decided, uncomfortably, to put off for another day telling Thomas the news of their impending departure. It was not quite urgent yet.

"I see Jackson's barn has burned down," he said after reading a few more paragraphs. "We'll have a walk up there on Saturday to see the damage."

"I know about that," said Thomas eagerly. "Phil Swanson said at school today that Donald Justice done it. They were fighting and that's when Donnie fell and bled his nose."

"*Did* it," said Patrick automatically, "and *made his nose bleed.*"

Then it came to him that such lessons were pointless. Soon he and Thomas would not need to speak any sort of English at all. He was weary and his weariness showed in his face, making him look younger and more vulnerable.

"Write it down anyway," he said. "It is all part of the account."

Thomas eyed his father quizzically. At that moment he felt suddenly afraid, as if his father knew something and was not telling. But no more was said.

 At bedtime Patrick came to tuck him up and put out the light.

"*Nallytan, Tonitheen ban,*" he said, gently stroking the dark hair back from the boy's forehead.

"*Nallytan, Vateelin mesht,*" said Thomas, using the one phrase he remembered from the language of the Other Place.

It will all come back to him, thought Vateelin as he closed the bedroom door. There was much that, of necessity, Tonitheen had forgotten; but what is forgotten can soon be recalled. Till then, they would be Patrick and Thomas, ordinary, unnoticeable inhabitants of Earth.

Chapter 3

Mrs. Dalrymple

Without Mrs. Dalrymple life would not have been so comfortable for the Derwents.

They had arrived in Belthorp five years before, later than expected and somewhat bewildered by delays and detours. This turned out to be for the best. In fact, a day later would have been even better. Whoever had arranged for their home to be furnished had failed to meet their deadline. So the Derwents had entered an empty house and spent their first night sleeping on the floor, the father hopefully reassuring his young son that the system would not fail them—the furniture would be there next day. And, surprisingly, it was.

The Derwents first met their new neighbor as they passed each other in the doorway of the village post office. They introduced themselves and then stood talking on the pavement, just across the way from Merrivale, the terrace of stone cottages with tiny front gardens and white-framed windows that was now home to all of them.

"I see you've moved in next door to me," said Mrs. Dalrymple, nodding over toward her own house. A furniture van was still parked there, the removal men just closing up the tailboard and preparing to leave.

Patrick smiled quite shyly. By his side stood Thomas, small, dark, and slightly built. Father and son did not resemble one another. Patrick was tall and broad-shouldered. His eyes were blue-gray, his hair thick, springy, and very light brown.

This lack of a resemblance was something that their new neighbor glancingly remarked upon.

"He'll take after his mother, I think," she said, smiling down at the six-year-old.

Patrick realized what she meant and said softly, "His mother died when he was a baby, but, yes, there is a likeness."

"Oh, I am sorry," said Mrs. Dalrymple in the same soft tone. "Had I thought, I would not have been so tactless."

Thomas was looking at the cobblestones beneath his feet, edging the toe of one sandal round the grooves and taking no notice of the grown-ups above him. It was only their third day in this place and everything was still a wonder to him.

Patrick noted his son's lack of interest in their conversation and was glad of it.

"You couldn't know, Mrs. Dalrymple," he said. "It happened a long time ago. Please don't worry."

Stella Dalrymple found herself feeling sorry for them. A motherless child, a young widower, together in strange surroundings. Stella was a widow herself, childless and living alone. But she had been born in Belthorp and had lived in her cottage at number 12 Merrivale for over twenty years, ever since her husband's death had brought her home to the village of her birth. Life had left her neither poor nor lonely. That is the prize for being self-sufficient. Yet there is always something left over, a wish to give.

The newcomers at number 13 both seemed to her to be in need of mothering.

"If I can be of any help," she said, "you know where I am."

Thomas caught Mrs. Dalrymple's words and looked up doubtfully at his father. The expression seemed somehow useful. Things that were possible to know must also be possible *not* to know.

"I don't know where I am," he said, as if trying out the words for size.

He looked so serious and so sweet as he spoke that both the grown-ups laughed lightly, and Patrick stooped to take one hand in his.

"You'll soon get used to us," said their new neighbor. "This is Belthorp, not Timbuctu."

Patrick and Mrs. Dalrymple went on talking for what seemed ages. Thomas grew impatient and then had a real need to go indoors. He looked up at his father and wondered shyly what to say, then settled on what he thought best.

"Say goodbye to the lady," he whispered urgently,

hitching on one foot and squeezing his father's hand tightly.

Mrs. Dalrymple heard him and laughed.

"I think your son's trying to tell you something," she said. "We'll have to talk again."

"I'm sure we will," said Patrick. "I look forward to it."

Over the next five years, Belthorp was Thomas Derwent's whole world and Stella Dalrymple became one of the most loved and most important people in it. She was older than his father but not grandmotherly. Her coppery, wavy hair had little trace of gray in it and her kind face was no more than lightly lined.

Within a fortnight of the Derwents' moving into number 13 Merrivale, she had become child minder and home help to the family next door; for a family is a family even if there are only two persons in it. It was she who turned their house into a warm and friendly home.

Her new job suited her very well. It did not interfere with her part-time job at Shotten Plastics, where she worked in the office, mornings only. The Derwents needed her in the afternoons and early evening. The arrangement, at Patrick's insistence, was formalized. "Fair's fair," he had said with his usual shy smile.

So Mrs. Dalrymple acquired an extra income, though that was not a prime concern. Above all, she found joy in the work. The Derwents in turn could not but appreciate the treasure that they had found. Mrs. Dalrymple was no fussy-body, harassing and disturbing them. She was cool, calm, and very efficient.

The first time she brought Thomas home from school and sat him down at the table in her own neat house to give him tea was something she would never forget. The little boy's chatter was so . . . imaginative! For a six-year-old, he possessed some very strange ideas. Mrs. Dalrymple put it down to things he must have seen on TV.

"How do you like Belthorp now?" she said as they sat together at table.

"It's different," said Thomas. "Did you know I was a river? And there's another boy at school who's a river. His name's Mickey Trent. And we both join up into another river."

A quick thought process made sense of this. Derwent . . . Trent.

"And you both flow into the Ouse!" said Mrs. Dalrymple, smiling.

"Yes!" said Thomas, giving her a look of wonder. "How did you know that?"

"Oh," said Mrs. Dalrymple, "there's lots of things I know! And I'm always ready to learn lots more."

Thomas liked that. He decided as he ate his home-made scones, which had cream and jam in them, that he very much liked Mrs. Dalrymple. He liked her house with its dark polished furniture and the plants on the windowsill. He liked the meal she had made for him at the table with its shining white cloth. He liked the log fire that crackled in the hearth. Above all, he liked the kindness he saw in Mrs. Dalrymple's eyes.

"It's nice here," he said. "I'm glad, I'm really, really glad, we came."

Mrs. Dalrymple was not an exceptionally nosy woman, rather the reverse; but by way of conversation she said, "And where did you live before?"

"A long, *long* way from here," said Thomas. "Coming here was very exciting, very, very exciting."

Mrs. Dalrymple laughed at the eagerness of his expression. "Sounds like a story," she said.

"It is! It is!" said Thomas. "It's a wonderful story, the best one I know. We came in a spaceship. But it was little, little, little . . ."

Thomas cupped his hand as if it were holding a ball. His fingers were sticky with jam and there was a dot of cream on his chin. A small, slim six-year-old with a fine, sensitive face, he looked the picture of innocence. But he was about to tell his new friend what she could only regard as an enormous whopper. Or, being kind, a tale displaying a child's most glorious imagination.

"And when we went in," he said in a rush of words, "we got tiny and everything inside was tiny, but we didn't know that because we were tiny as well. And when we came out, we got big, big, big . . ."

He stood up, spread his arms, and puffed out his chest to demonstrate.

"And our cases got big, big, big and everything we had brought with us got big again. Then my father unpacked his wallet of money, and we left the spaceship in the soil because it was too heavy to move, and we went to a station and we got some tickets, and we got on two trains—not at the same time, one first, then another. And that's how we came here. My father said it was all as-a-range. Except the spaceship landed in the wrong place. And the marvelous bit was going round and round the moon twice, but that was a mistake as well.''

Mrs. Dalrymple laughed again, affectionately. Her hazel eyes twinkled as she looked across the table at his solemn face. For that moment the child was so engrossed in the tale he was telling that it seemed as if he really believed it.

"Does your father know this story?" she said gently.

"Course he does," said Thomas, looking puzzled. "He was there. And we looked in the shop windows we passed with mirrors and we saw what we looked like."

By now they had finished tea. Mrs. Dalrymple cleared the table and the two of them went into her little sitting room and settled down to watch some children's television. *I'd better watch this,* she thought. *I obviously need to keep up to date!*

"Your son's a very bright little boy," said Mrs. Dalrymple to Patrick when he came to collect him. Thomas was up in the bathroom washing his hands, so there was no danger of giving him too conceited a view of himself.

"I think he is," said Patrick, smiling, "but I could be prejudiced!"

She then told him the spaceship story.

"I've heard that one before," said Patrick with a laugh. "I suppose it's more interesting than saying we came from Hemel Hempstead!"

Five years on, the story remained unfinished, and Stella Dalrymple never found out anything about her neighbors' past. That didn't matter. After all, she never told them about some years of her own past, spent in a very different place. The sadness of losing her husband was not something she talked about. The present was enough, and the present was mainly joyful.

Chapter 4

Belthorp Primary

The whole of Belthorp was in a basin surrounded by hill farms. From the windows of Belthorp Primary School the children could see sheep grazing in a not totally unspoiled countryside. To the east, at the foot of Shotten Hill, was a grim-looking modern factory. To the northwest, the pit heap of an abandoned colliery was slowly being reclaimed. Most of the classrooms were on the north side of the school. The south side looked out onto the playground and the village street.

It was the day after the fight.

Mickey Trent's "flu" had cleared enough for him to return to school. He and Thomas were leaning against the railings beside the school gate. Mickey was overweight but not a soft, fat boy. His big bones supported the extra weight comfortably and he was not at all flabby. The makings of a good fighter, not a bad mate to have by your side, though such a thought never occurred to Thomas Derwent. He never knew how many times Mickey's strength had saved him from the usual bullying such a slight, clever boy might expect to suffer.

Mickey had been by Thomas's side from the first day they met. Six-year-old Thomas was the newcomer. Mickey had been at the school for over a year. It was Miss Crosbie, the class teacher at the time, who set them up as allies. She it was who called them "the two rivers." *The Derwent and the Trent, you know, are tributaries of the River Ouse.* It was as good as being blood brothers! And what a nice way to make a new boy feel at home! Thomas soon proved to be much cleverer than his friend, but that was no disadvantage. They worked quite happily as a team. Besides, Thomas was only clever at sums and spelling and things like that. It didn't stop him being very gullible, and Mickey could usually put him straight.

"Did Donnie *really* set fire to Jackson's barn?" Thomas asked his friend as they stood waiting for the bell to ring. "My father read about the fire in the paper."

"Don't you go saying that," said Mickey, horrified. "Of course he didn't! It was just Phil's idea of a joke. You know what those two are like! Donnie Justice would no more think of setting fire to a barn than of flying to the moon!"

"Remember, I've been there," said Thomas quite seriously. "Like I told you, we flew round it twice on our way to Earth. I still remember how crummy it

looked, nowhere near as good as this place. I don't
know why *anybody* would want to go to it."

Mickey laughed. Thomas told some fantastic stories,
always had. They made you think of doing things! Like
flying . . . Both boys then sprouted wings that were
really arms and flew round and round the yard, dip-
ping and diving, till the bell went and spoiled their
game.

Miss Kershaw had a headache. It made her cross
and irritable. The children streaming into the
room were as noisy as children always are, scraping
chairs, bumping about with school bags and settling
down a bit like an orchestra tuning up before the con-
cert.

"Please be quiet," said Miss Kershaw. She felt like
asking for mercy but eleven-year-olds are not famed for
being merciful. It helped that she was young and
pretty, but it is a rare child who can really see a teacher
as a vulnerable human being!

"Sit down," she said firmly, "all of you, and stop
that chatter. Today is going to be a very, very quiet
day."

At that moment an airplane swooped low over the
school on its way to the RAF training base and
drowned out her voice. At the back of the classroom,
Donald Justice and Philip Swanson stamped their feet
briefly and giggled.

Miss Kershaw smiled wanly.

"It will be as quiet a day as we can make it," she said. "There is enough noise on this planet without our adding to it."

Thomas always liked it when Miss Kershaw said "this planet." To him it seemed like some sort of recognition. Miss Kershaw was a friend of the Earth. Though at that moment she did not feel particularly friendly toward anything or anybody.

"Now then," she said, holding up the sheaf of cards she had in her hand, "I have prepared a task card for each of you. You will carry out your own special task in silence. If you have any questions, come quietly and ask me."

"Can we do them in any order, Miss Kershaw?" said Rosie Bigwood, seeing even at the age of eleven that the system was ripe for chaos. It could end up with lots of people trying to grab the same card! That might be fun.

"No," said Miss Kershaw sharply, knowing exactly what Rosie had in mind. "You must do them in the order given and return each card to the table before you start on the next task. And do it quietly."

Or at least that is what she probably said. Her final words were lost as another plane passed noisily overhead.

"Funny how there's always two of them," said Philip in a voice that was louder than he intended. He had thought the plane's noise would drown out his words, but the plane had gone before he got them out. Miss Kershaw glared at him.

"Our spaceship was much quieter than that," said Thomas in a whisper to his friend. "It could travel faster than sound without even making a bang."

"Give over," said Mickey, nudging his elbow. "We'll play it outside later. Miss Kershaw's getting vexed. She looks to me as if she's got a bad head."

After that, the class settled down to a hum of quiet work. Each child was working seriously within his or her own scope. It would have needed deliberate malice to spoil the lesson and the children of Belthorp Primary were not deliberately malicious, whatever else they might be.

Thomas was on to his fourth task—drawing and labeling figures with three, four, five, six, and seven sides—when his mind strayed into thoughts of what his father had hinted at the night before. Yet it was not so much what he'd said as how he'd said it and how he'd looked. Thomas shivered as the thought came to him that perhaps this life of theirs was ending. He stopped work and his dark eyes brimmed with tears.

Miss Kershaw noticed. Her head was clearing. The lesson was going well, and she had time to notice Thomas Derwent faltering and fighting tears.

"What's wrong, Thomas?" she said quietly, coming close to him.

"I don't know," said Thomas in a very low voice. "What does dying feel like? I don't ever want to die."

Miss Kershaw bent over him as if inspecting his work. At these last words she held back a smile.

"You really needn't worry about that just yet," she

said solemnly. "Finish your work. You're doing very well. At this rate, you'll win *three* merit marks!"

Thomas looked up at her.

"I want to stay here," he said. "I don't want to go away."

Miss Kershaw remembered that Thomas and his father were newcomers to the village—or had been five years ago, and that was pretty much the same.

"Is your father being transferred elsewhere?" she said. Mr. Derwent, they all understood, worked for a multinational chemical company, commuting each day the forty miles to town. And multinationals, so she assumed, can move their people around.

"I don't know," said Thomas bleakly. "He hasn't said."

The school day ended well. A fully recovered Miss Kershaw gave out the parts for the Christmas play. Emma was Mary, Donnie was Joseph, and the rest of the cast included Mickey Trent as the angel Gabriel and Thomas Derwent in the role of the youngest shepherd.

When Thomas came home from school looking thoroughly miserable, Stella felt real concern. She settled him down to his tea and sat beside him at the table. It was a while before she came to the point. She knew not to rush him. Thomas sat silently eating his food, as if to do so were a great effort.

"Is something wrong, Thomas?" she said as she

poured herself a second cup of tea. "Has something happened at school?"

Thomas took a big bite out of his sandwich and tried hard not to cry. Tears gathered rebelliously on his dark lashes.

"What *is* the matter?" said Stella, immediately aware of the body's distress. "You can tell me. I'll see to it, whatever it is. Troubles are best shared."

Thomas put down the remains of the sandwich and looked across at her wretchedly.

"Has my father said anything to you about us going away?" he said.

"No," said Stella. "Not a word. And if you were going, he'd be sure to say. He's much too nice and too polite to leave without giving me notice."

"And you would tell me?" said Thomas.

"Of course I would," she said, then leaned over and gripped his arm. "But Thomas, Thomas, please listen to me. If you were leaving Belthorp, your father would tell you properly himself. He would never, ever upset you like this. What put the idea into your head?"

"Something," said Thomas awkwardly. "Nothing. Just a feeling. And I don't want to go. I like it here. This is my home."

"Well, you ask him about it," said Stella. "Wait till you are alone and tell him exactly what's worrying you and why. Bringing things out into the open is good for children and for grown-ups too. Hidden worries hurt more."

* * *

24

By the time Patrick came home, something had happened to distract Thomas's attention from those hidden cares. It was snowing. Heavy flakes were falling and rapidly covering the ground.

"We'll still go for our walk tomorrow," said Thomas eagerly. "To see Jackson's barn. You said we could. And I'd love to go walking in the snow, finding parts that nobody's been to."

"I don't see why not," said his father. "Explorers have to start somewhere!"

Chapter 5

A Walk in the Snow

"Vandals," said Patrick sadly.

Thomas looked at him uncertainly. They were standing on the edge of Jackson's field. Father and son were both clad for the weather—anoraks, scarves, gloves, and Wellington boots. All around was snow, covering the fields, lying heavy on the hedges, glistening in a weak winter sun that somehow gave everything shadows that were yellowy brown.

The only sharp color in the whole landscape was the blackened skeleton of Jackson's barn. The roof appeared to be still intact, but nothing else remained except four charred uprights whose branched tops held the roof in place.

Patrick saw his son's puzzled look and added, "No, son, it was no one from *your* school. These would be real vandals, older and stupider. Remember why Donnie was ready to fight his friend, even for joking about it? He had nothing to do with this. I doubt if anyone will ever know who did. It's hard to imagine who would want to destroy something so sturdy and so old. It's a bit of history."

"The roof's not gone," said Thomas hopefully.

"Yes," said Patrick. "And they'll probably save it. But that's no thanks to the idiots who started the fire."

"Will the owls come back?" said Thomas.

"I would think so," said his father. "All creatures tend to return to their own base. As we shall to ours."

"And our base is Belthorp," said Thomas firmly. "Let's go home now. Stella will have our dinner ready."

He looked anxiously at his father, willing him not to contradict his words. *I am Thomas Derwent, and Belthorp is my home.* He shivered and turned to face downhill toward the village in the valley.

Patrick felt guilty for keeping so much to himself. He made up his mind to broach the subject of their departure. He had to begin somewhere and time was running out.

"We don't really belong here," he said, one hand resting on his son's shoulder. "You must never forget that. We are here with a job to do. When the job is finished, we will be going home to Ormingat."

Thomas said nothing. Instead he scrunched his boots into the snow and kept his head down. He clung to the possibility that their leaving was not imminent, that perhaps it could be delayed, delayed indefinitely. He rooted round in his brain for arguments to persuade his father to stay put.

27

"Stella couldn't come to Ormingat," he said. "Stella has never heard of Ormingat."

"I should hope not," said Patrick. "You know the rules. You must never, except in the *direst of circumstances,* tell anyone your real name or your real place of origin. Those words are keys and someday you might need them."

Thomas did not understand, but neither did he feel the urge to question. He did not want to know anything about "the direst of circumstances." The whole idea was too hard for Mickey Trent's best friend, even if he *was* always top for sums and reading. If he had known how to put it into words, he might have said, *Look here, I'm Thomas Derwent. I go to Belthorp Primary and Miss Kershaw's just given me a part in the end-of-term play.* That's *important. I don't want to know about anything else.*

Yet that was not quite accurate. There was one thing he wanted to know here and now. There was one thing he was conscious of waiting to be told. He looked at his father expectantly.

Patrick hesitated but said nothing.

They walked on in silence. Darkness fell and, one by one, stars brightened in the blackness of the sky.

They passed the first street of houses in the village. The streetlamps were giving their own special light to the snow. In the distance, children on the village green, just beyond Merrivale, were shouting faintly and throwing snowballs.

It was Thomas who decided to break the deadlock. He had to ask the question, even though he was deeply afraid of what the answer might be.

He stood still and turned to face his father. He had only the faintest idea of how orders might come and from whom.

"When have we got to go back?" he said. "Have you had word somehow? It's not fair to hint and hint and not tell me what's really going to happen."

Patrick nodded. It was a fair enough complaint.

"You're right," he said. "I'll have to tell you everything. But let's wait now till we are indoors and settled down to dinner. Then, after Stella goes next door, we'll talk."

Stella was waiting in the cottage. The table was set for two and as soon as she heard the key in the door she lifted the casserole out of the oven and began ladling the food onto plates. The kettle was boiling. There was tea in the pot. Here was comfort after a cold, cold walk.

"You must be perished," she said as they came into the room, bringing a chill with them. "Come and sit down. The dinner's all ready."

She noticed that something other than the chill of winter was hovering in the air. Then she too began to wonder whether Thomas's fears had some basis in fact. *I hope not,* she thought. *I do hope not.*

Thomas watched her as she prepared to go. Never to see Stella again would break his heart. Everything about her seemed to him so perfect—her hazel eyes, her bright smile, even the autumn colors she nearly always wore. The children at school had mothers.

Secretly Thomas thought of Stella as his own special mother, though he knew she would never be his father's wife. It was more as if she were mother to both of them.

"I'll be going now, Patrick," said Stella. "Good night. Good night, Thomas. See you tomorrow."

"Yes," said Thomas emphatically, and he put his arms round Stella's neck and gave her a strong hug. To her this was another indication, a sign that something was not quite as it should be. Six-year-old Thomas had often hugged her. By the age of eight he had come to regard such demonstrations as babyish. Stella returned the hug but had the tact not to comment.

"Good night," she said, "and God bless."

Chapter 6

Nothing but
the Truth

After Stella left, Thomas looked anxiously at his father, waiting for him to begin the promised talk. But Patrick was still working out what to say and, more importantly, what not to say. His son must not know too much too soon.

"Do y'think the snow will last till Christmas?" said Thomas at last. He could have been any boy hoping that Christmas day would look just like something out of a storybook. But it was a trick question. Thomas was consciously probing, and Patrick knew immediately what he was up to.

"I don't think so," said his father very deliberately, "but if it does, we will not be here to see it. That is what you want to know, isn't it?"

Thomas put his fork down noisily on the table. For the first time ever he felt some understanding of what made Belthorp children stand and fight. It was something he had never been trained to do, and it was totally against his nature.

"We go *before Christmas?*" he said, outraged. "You should have told me sooner. How long have you known?"

Patrick sighed and knew the time had come for all those long explanations.

"I am sorry, Thomas, truly sorry. I have known the date of our departure ever since we came here. It was one of the things that I was not at liberty to tell you. It was essential to the experiment."

"*One* of the things?" said Thomas sharply. "What else do I not know?"

"Not a lot," said Patrick. "Just bits and pieces. Everything kept back from you has been kept back of necessity. Now I can tell you more, and I *want* to tell you more. I don't enjoy keeping secrets."

Thomas suddenly did not want to hear any more, not just yet. Another thought had come to mind, a far more important, Belthorp thought. He was not just pretending to belong here. He had acclimatized. Environment had won out.

"I can't go before the end of term," he said in near-panic. "There's the Nativity play. I'm the youngest shepherd. Get in touch with them, whoever they are. Tell them your work's not finished. Tell them you need another year."

"I can't get in touch with anyone yet," said Patrick. "I have had no contact with Ormingat since we came here. That's how it is. That's how it was meant to be. Besides, the work is yours even more than mine. You have supplied five years' data on what it is like to be a boy in an English village. *You* have lived the life and written the accounts. That is what we are here for."

"But why do they want to know?" said Thomas, thinking of all the ordinary things he had written about, not things really worth putting into a book. He knew that, even if he was only eleven. "What use is it to them?"

"Something else I can't really explain yet," said his father. "It is to do with things that might happen perhaps a hundred years or more from now."

Thomas gave him a look of wonder. He was an eleven-year-old boy to whom centuries were history. Time extending into the future went not much further than the day after tomorrow.

"I don't understand," he said, struggling with the idea. "A hundred years is a very long time."

"A thousand years is even longer," said Patrick cryptically, and at that Thomas gave up all effort to make sense of it. They ate for a while in silence, each in his own way perplexed.

If anything, it was even worse for Patrick than for Thomas. He was facing the awareness that what he had done in allowing the experiment was something he should perhaps never have undertaken. *I was too young to know,* he thought. *Keldu was not there to protect our son.* They *should have warned me better.*

Now there was no choice. There was nothing for it but to carry it through to the end. Patrick could not and would not be disloyal to Ormingat no matter how sorely tempted he might be. So he would have to talk freely to Thomas about what was happening and what would happen. He would have to try to make him understand.

"Have you ever told anyone about your journal?" he said at length, coming at the subject from an angle.

"I told Mickey once," said Thomas defensively. "You didn't tell me not to tell anybody."

"And what did Mickey say?" said his father.

"He didn't really believe it. He thought all I was doing was keeping a diary and he said I was daft for bothering. He didn't believe that I *had* to do it. He never believes anything I tell him. He loves to hear about the spaceship, but he thinks I am just making it up."

"That is why you were allowed to tell," said his father. "It was well thought out. The only things I taught you never to repeat were our real names and the name of Ormingat. It was all that could be expected of a six-year-old. Other things you did not know and were not told."

"Like the date of leaving?" said Thomas resentfully.

"Yes," said Patrick, "and the location of the spaceship."

"We left it in some soil," said Thomas triumphantly, "underneath a sort of monument, a big stone monument. I remember that, so there!"

"And in what town is the monument, Thomas?" said his father, smiling for the first time in this strained conversation.

Thomas frowned and tried with all his might to remember anything at all about the landing site. He could see it quite clearly: a large tree, green grass, a city full of shops. Something like a castle high up on a hill. Only the name of the city escaped him.

"The spaceship came down," he said, "but it was the wrong place and we had to get the train. And the spaceship looked like a golf ball, though I didn't know that then. We came out of it somehow and grew to the size of things on Earth. Then we walked along a main street and looked in mirrors and that was where I saw myself for the very first time."

"That's good," said Patrick. "I didn't know you remembered so much. What about the time aboard the spaceship—our three years in space?"

Thomas shook his head.

"Not much," he said, struggling. "Videos of some sort. Paper and writing, printing *Thomas Derwent* in capital letters on sheets of paper. Then reading books about Janet and John. And playing games and learning when to sleep. Why did I have to learn to sleep?"

"We live differently," said Patrick softly. *"Verleel mongoo, Tonitheen. Vateelin millistig thent."*

Thomas struggled to make sense of his father's words, but all he could make out were the names: Tonitheen and Vateelin.

"I don't understand the Ormingat words," he said crossly. "You must know I don't. I recognize our other names, but nothing else."

"You will learn," said his father. "You are a good scholar. In the three years it will take to travel home again, you will come to know the language of Ormingat as well as you know English—better. It is, after all,

35

your mother tongue. You began to speak it in your infancy."

"So we really are leaving?" said Thomas. "Leaving before Christmas?"

"We are," said father. "But now you have heard enough for one night. Finish your dinner and then get ready for bed. Tomorrow there is much more I need to tell you. It's not easy for me, Thomas. It's not easy for either of us. Leaving is a new idea for you. I want you to get used to it."

There was something about Patrick's words that told Thomas that it would be in vain to ask anything else just now. Besides, he wanted to be alone. Getting used to the idea of leaving Belthorp would be very, very difficult.

Patrick went to tuck his son in, as usual, and say good night. The boy looked as if he were sleeping.

Patrick bent over him.

"Nallytan, Tonitheen ban," he said quietly.

The boy stirred, yawned, then murmured, *"Nallytan, Vateelin mesht."*

Chapter 7

Conspirators

On Sundays Patrick always made a proper English breakfast. Thomas went early to church with Stella and shared the meal with his father after he returned.

The next morning being Sunday, Thomas got up later than on weekdays and had, as usual, to wash and dress straightaway so as not to keep Stella waiting. There was no time to continue the discussion of the night before.

Patrick was in the kitchen making a pot of coffee when Thomas came downstairs.

The doorbell rang and simultaneously a key was turned in the front-door lock.

"Here's Stella come to fetch you," Patrick said. "We'll talk later."

It was the beginning of what felt to both of them uncomfortably like a conspiracy.

* * *

The congregation sang "All Things Bright and Beautiful" and then, with regard to the season, "See amid the Winter's Snow." Outside the little church, the snow in fact was rapidly melting and would soon be gone. Thomas stood up and sat down in all the right places, but his mind was definitely elsewhere.

It was a relief when Stella left him at his own front gate.

"Lunch at three-thirty," she said. "See you then."

She knew that Thomas hardly heard what she was saying. Stella Dalrymple was very perceptive but also very patient. There was a mystery, but mysteries tend to be far less important than children think. Lunch would be at three-thirty in her house as usual. Perhaps there would be some indication then of what was troubling Thomas, perhaps there would not.

When Thomas went into the house, his father was busily setting the table for breakfast.

"The snow's nearly gone, I see," said Patrick.

"There's still plenty up on the hills," said Thomas, "but it's all turned to slush in the village."

They sat down at the table and looked at each other awkwardly, neither quite knowing how to begin.

Thomas ate his cereal in what became almost a sulky silence. Then he said abruptly, "Well, when are we going? And you haven't told Stella yet and I think that's horrible."

"I'll tell Stella today," said Patrick. "I'm not happy about that either. I would like to have told her months ago, but it wouldn't have been wise. Your reports had to be kept going for as long as possible. You had to forget that this was not our permanent home."

Thomas was angry. It was an alien emotion, one he had learned to recognize in others but till now had hardly experienced for himself.

"That was deception," he said, using one of the words he had learned from his father, a word he valued as sounding much more important than simply "telling lies." "I thought, I have always thought, that *we* did not deceive. It is what you have taught me."

"There was no deception," said his father defensively. "I always told you the truth, but not all of the truth."

"And what will you tell Stella?" asked Thomas, seeing the flaw, the point where anything but deception would surely be impossible. "You can't tell *her* the truth."

Patrick clasped both hands on the table in front of him.

"I will never be other than honest with you," he said, "but you are right, I shall be forced to deceive Stella. I'll somehow imply that I have been transferred to Winnipeg. I'll tell her as little as possible but whatever I do say will be less than true. That is very, very difficult. I don't want to do it, but the only alternative is to leave without a word. And that, I believe, would be even worse."

Patrick took away the empty cereal bowls and put down plates of bacon, eggs, and mushrooms.

The question that had begun this discussion was still unanswered.

"When *do* we leave? What day? What time? How do we travel?" said Thomas, growing impatient.

"We leave Belthorp by train on the morning of the eighteenth of December," said his father.

"So I *will* miss the Nativity play," said Thomas.

He was not an astronaut, nothing like it. He was an eleven-year-old schoolboy and had been given the part of the youngest shepherd with a lamb to carry as a gift for the Baby Jesus. It was not a big part, but he wanted so much to do it. Patrick saw the disappointment in his face.

"I'm sorry," he said. "Truly sorry. We'll be on the train to Casselton then. There is nothing, absolutely nothing I can do about it. These dates and times were arranged years ago. We need time on the spaceship before we quit Earth and head off for home. There will be a course to plot and news to gather. Eight years is a long time."

"And then?" said Thomas.

"If all goes well," said Patrick, "we shall begin our real journey at midnight on the twenty-sixth—the day after Christmas. No significance in that. No one on Ormingat has a special regard for Boxing Day or, if you prefer it, the Feast of Stephen!"

"What do I tell Mickey?" said Thomas as he thought of the only friend who really mattered. "I've never told him a lie. He's my best friend."

"That is why I can't tell you the exact location of the spaceship. Place names are dangerous. What you do not know you cannot tell. And if you tell Mickey the truth *as you know it,* there is little risk of anything going

wrong. Remember how much he enjoys your stories—
and how little he really believes."

Thomas looked across at his father. Breakfast continued as if everything were normal. Thomas, without thinking, spread marmalade on his toast. Patrick
poured them each a cup of coffee, half filling Thomas's
with milk.

"I shall ring the school tomorrow," said Patrick,
"and tell the headmistress that you will be leaving. I
shall say that you are not happy about going and that I
would prefer her to ask you no questions."

"You've thought of everything," said Thomas resentfully. "Will you tell Stella to say nothing to me?"

"I won't need to," said Patrick, rather shamefaced.
"She is discretion itself. If she asks you anything about
Canada, you will tell her the same as you tell Mickey—
the absolute truth—that you are flying in a golf ball to
your home in outer space. Then she will conclude that
you are fantasizing again and will ask no more. She will
simply believe that you are too upset to talk about it."

Stella Dalrymple might be one of the most perfect of human beings, but that did not prevent
her being both upset and annoyed when Patrick broke
the news. They were seated at the dinner table and had
just finished their soup. A pause between courses, a
meal never hurried and usually happy.

"Leaving in two weeks' time!" she said. "Leaving for
good! You might have told me before now, Patrick. I
don't mean because I work for you. I never think of

41

myself as your employee—you have never made me feel that way. I am first and foremost your friend and neighbor. I will be very sad to see you go. It would have been kinder to have given me more time to get used to the idea."

"I told you, Father," said Thomas vigorously. "Didn't I tell you? You should have given both of us more time. I don't want to go, Stella. This is where I want to live for always."

At this, Stella had some notion of what had been happening next door and some idea of why Thomas had seemed distressed before he even knew of the move. She removed the soup plates and carried them to the kitchen corner.

"You must have your reasons, I suppose," she said with a sigh. "Did your company give you such short notice, Patrick?"

Like everyone in the village, Stella assumed that Patrick was an executive with the chemical company in Casselton. He had never said so, but it was a natural assumption—a newcomer, a professional, transferred from Hemel Hempstead, was it?

Patrick looked at Stella and shook his head. He was unused to lying. The big lie was rehearsed. Smaller lies were still a stumbling block.

"I have known for some time," he said clumsily, "but I kept it to myself. Perhaps I couldn't face up to it. I love Belthorp too. I would like to stay here longer."

What Stella thought at that moment she too kept to herself. It was not her place to criticize. She even regretted her initial outburst.

42

"I'm sorry," she said, looking directly at Patrick. "If I have said anything to upset you, blame it on the fact that I really shall miss both of you. Thomas has been like a son to me."

Dinner plates were brought to the table. Stella was serving the meat, large, thin slices of pork. She smiled wistfully as she passed a plate to Thomas.

Thomas gulped and reddened. Patrick also had a childlike sadness in his face. Clearly neither of them was happy to go. Stella looked at them both with growing pity. One son? Two sons. Patrick never seemed to her to be quite grown-up.

"You must not forget me," she said gently. "You must both write to me from Winnipeg and I shall write to you and tell you all the village gossip."

Lunch was proceeding as if nothing untoward were happening. Stella, as she spoke, was ladling vegetables onto Thomas's plate.

"It's pork this week," said Thomas quickly, looking down at his plate. "I really do like pork."

"Have some applesauce," said Patrick, passing his son the dish.

Stella was too busy to notice that her promise to write was being ignored. The conspirators experienced a feeling of relief.

Chapter 8

End of Term

It was the Monday of Thomas's last week on Earth.

He had just told Mickey that he would be leaving the school on Thursday, a day before everybody else would be breaking up for the Christmas holidays. Then, with his father, he would be traveling to their spaceship and setting off for the distant planet in another solar system that was his own true home.

"You're not," said Mickey scornfully. "I know you're not. The play's on Friday and you're the youngest shepherd. That's your sheep in the corner over there."

The sheep was a little woolly lamb brought in by Mandy Maynard, the quietest girl in the class, if not the school. It was beautifully clean, if somewhat short of fleece, and it was sitting on the long brown box in the corner by the blackboard.

Thomas looked across at it and felt near to tears.

At that moment Miss Kershaw brought the class to attention and the day began.

Badly.

"Now," said the teacher, "I think we should have a rehearsal for Friday's play. There's just one little complication. Thomas will be leaving us on Thursday. So we'll need another youngest shepherd. Mandy, since you were kind enough to bring the lamb, would you like the part?"

Mandy blushed scarlet and shook her head.

"I'd like you to do it, Mandy," said Miss Kershaw, smiling, "and the lamb would probably like it too. Give it a try, eh? You won't have very much to say."

"I can say the words for her," said Donnie helpfully. "I can say, 'Look, Mary. Look what the youngest shepherd's brung you.' "

"We'll see," said Miss Kershaw diplomatically. "Mandy will probably want to say her own words once she's got used to the idea. The headdress helps. People are never shy when they're wearing a headdress."

And while all this was going on, there was thunder at the table by the window, the table Thomas and Mickey shared. Mickey had pointedly turned his back on Thomas so that all Thomas could see of him was the shoulder of his red jersey.

"Face the front, Mickey," said Miss Kershaw when she noticed.

Mickey turned to the front again, glowered sideways at Thomas, and said nothing.

By break, Miss Kershaw and most of the others in

the room were aware that the impossible had happened. Mickey had fallen out with his best friend and was not speaking to him.

When the bell rang, the other children filed out, but Miss Kershaw kept those two behind.

"Come on," she said, looking at Mickey, "what's it all about?"

"I don't ever want to speak to him again," said Mickey, looking utterly miserable. "He tells lies."

Thomas blanched. His dark eyes were darker than ever in the little white face.

"I don't," he said, then looked accusingly at Mickey. "And you promised never to tell any of my secrets."

"You didn't tell me you were really leaving," said Mickey. "I thought it was just a game. And you haven't told me where you're really going."

"He's really going to Winnipeg," said Miss Kershaw. "It's in Canada, Mickey. I can show you on the map."

She took a school atlas from the pile on the table and flipped through to the right page.

"There," she said. "Winnipeg is in Manitoba and Manitoba is a province in Canada."

"It's a long way away," said Mickey, "but it's not further than the moon."

"No," said Miss Kershaw, unsure what he was driving at.

"So why didn't he tell me where he was going? Why did he have to tell me lies?"

Tears began to slide down Thomas's cheeks.

Miss Kershaw noticed and said gently, "Wait outside the door for a minute or two, Thomas. I want a quiet word with Mickey. You two have always been friends. This is something we can put right, something we *must* put right."

Thomas went out reluctantly with backward, desperate glances at his friend.

"Now, Mickey," said Miss Kershaw as the door closed, "I won't ask you what this is all about. What I do want to say is this—Thomas is very upset about leaving. I don't know what lies you think he has told you, but if he is making up stories, maybe it's because he's unhappy."

"*I'm* unhappy," said Mickey. "I don't want him to go."

"If his dad goes, Mickey," said the teacher, "then he has no choice. You must see that. If your mam had to leave Belthorp, you couldn't stay here, now could you?"

"But I'd tell the truth about where I was going," said Mickey. "I wouldn't tell *him* I was flying into outer space."

Miss Kershaw found it difficult not to laugh but knew it was important to stay serious.

"If that's what he said, Mickey, I see no harm in it. He's upset about going and he wants to hide how upset he is. You are his very best friend. You can help to make it easier for him."

Mickey nodded miserably. He was still getting used to the idea that Thomas was really about to leave.

Miss Kershaw went to the door and brought Thomas back into the room.

"Now," she said, "I want you two to be friends

again. It's unheard-of for the two of you to quarrel. Go out for break now—and come back smiling!"

"I really am going to my own planet," said Thomas doggedly when they got outside. "It wasn't a lie at all. But if you like, we can pretend I'm going to Winnipeg. We can find out all sorts of things about Winnipeg and what I'll be doing when I get there."

Mickey was generous.

"No," he said. "If you want to play at going into outer space, we'll play that instead. It'll be more fun. We'll have a countdown and launchpads and things like that. Except when you really do go, I hope you'll not forget me. You could send postcards or something. And you might come back."

What Mickey called the rocket game kept the two friends going till Thursday teatime. They walked home together for the last time. As they reached Thomas's front door, Mickey awkwardly handed him a keyring with a tiny green plastic rocket on it.

"D day minus one," he said in a forced, false voice as he put the gift into Thomas's hand. "Reports to be sent back immediately on landing!"

Thomas took the keyring. Then, quite suddenly, he leaned towards his friend and whispered, "The planet I am going to is called Ormingat."

Mickey heard, and shivered from the nape of his neck right down to his toes.

Then Thomas ran into the house and lay on his bed and wept.

Mickey, left alone and puzzled, began to sneeze and was still sneezing when he reached home.

"Looks as if you're in for another cold," said Mrs. Trent anxiously. "Get yourself by the fire. I'll make you some hot lemon."

Chapter 9

The Journey to Casselton

"I don't want to go," said Thomas.

They were in the train traveling east to Casselton, from where they were supposedly going south to London to board a plane to Canada. The carriage was nearly empty. Patrick and Thomas faced each other across the table. Outside, fields and hedges hurried by, and snowcapped hills gave place to flat, bleak meadows.

On the table in front of him, Thomas had the game of travel Scrabble that Stella had given him for "now instead of Christmas." She had come with them to the station and seen them onto the train. Thomas did not hug her when they parted on the platform. The look he gave her was almost a reproach, as if somehow he had hoped that she would stop it happening. *She* hugged *him* and said quietly, "It'll be all right. You'll see."

The only other present Thomas took with him was the keyring with the tiny green plastic rocket on it.

Now, with the train drawing ever nearer to Casselton, Thomas had had time to think more seriously about where they were heading and how they were going to get there. He had left the past in Belthorp station; the present was here in the railway carriage; and the future was horribly close in a spaceship the size and shape of a golf ball.

Patrick looked across at him and said nothing.

"I mean it, Father. I don't want to go and I won't go," said Thomas.

"You can't say that," said Patrick. "That is something you are not allowed to say. Where I go, you go. You are mine."

His father's face, so fair and so unlike his own, took on a closed expression. Patrick was not finding the argument easy. He could see his son's point of view and he felt guilty.

Thomas grew angry.

"I am not yours," he said, tears starting to sting his eyes. "I am *mine* and I don't want to go in the spaceship and shrink little."

Then Patrick understood. It was not the longing to stay behind that was uppermost in Thomas's mind at that moment. It was the fear of going forward, like the fear some people have of flying, only worse. That was an an easier problem to tackle. At least it did not require him to take a very dubious moral standpoint.

"I'm sorry, Thomas," he said. "It was stupid of me

not to think how frightening this must be for you. And there's no shame in being afraid."

Thomas rubbed one hand over his eyes and looked at Patrick curiously.

"I *am* afraid," he said. "I really do remember coming out of the spaceship and growing big. I don't know how we did it. I was only six. It seemed exciting then. It always has seemed exciting, even though nobody would believe me. But to go little again is terrifying. It could go wrong, couldn't it? We might get stuck somewhere. The spaceship landed in the wrong place, and we *did* fly twice round the moon."

"That," said Patrick defensively, "was a simple error of navigation. Diminishing—which is the proper term for it—is well within our scope. Diminishing and then, when the time comes, increasing and becoming our proper shape and size."

The train stopped briefly at Chamfort, but no one came or left. The journey was almost at an end.

Thomas thought furiously, a twisting turmoil of thoughts.

"I don't know how it can be done," he said. "I've learned lots of things at school, but it's only in fairy stories that things change size and shape. Are we magic?"

Patrick smiled. Magic would be such a simple way to provide answers.

"No," he said. "I will try to explain, but I can't guarantee to manage it. First, you know that it is true, because you know that's how we came here."

Thomas nodded solemnly, conceding this as fact.

"Well," continued Patrick, "we were able to do that because our scientists have proceeded along different lines from those on Earth. Here they have a very firm grasp of the relativity of space and time. But they have not yet come to terms with the fact that size is cosmic illusion. Only their *poets* come anywhere near the concept of seeing things 'through the wrong end of the long telescope' or perceiving 'a world in a grain of sand.' Our *scientists* know that perception can be controlled."

Thomas partly understood; his experience of size change was enough to make it at least a familiar idea. But there were still problems unsolved and thoughts too hard for an eleven-year-old to grasp.

"How?" he said simply, trying to cut across all the long words. "How is it done?"

"They harness energy, just as on Earth," said Patrick. "Exactly how they achieve it, I don't really know. It is not my job to know. But the energy is stored within the sphere you call a golf ball and which we both know is really our spaceship. We touch one so-called dimple on the golf ball and the energy diminishes us and everything we are holding. We are, as it were, tuned to it. It draws us in, just as matter is supposed to be drawn into what scientists here call a black hole. Do you understand?"

Thomas looked from his dark Earth face into his father's blue-gray eyes. Did he understand? No, he most certainly did not.

"I don't understand black holes and energy," he said flatly. "It's like believing in Santa Claus. At one time I really believed in him. Now I don't."

Patrick put one hand across the table and grasped his son's delicate fingers.

"You needn't understand any of it," he said, "so long as you trust me. You are the most important person in my life. I would never, ever take you into harm's way."

Then there was an illusion indescribable of two beings closely akin exchanging loving thoughts. For a few moments everything in the carriage faded from sight, as if some strange aura surrounded the two of them. *As I am . . . so are you . . . passengers in space and time.* Words somehow echoed in the rhythm of the train.

"I do trust you, Vateelin *mesht*," said the boy.

"Then you will have no fear, Tonitheen," said his father. "*Leckejil, Tonitheen ban.* There is no need for fear."

The spell was broken when over the train's loudspeaker came the announcement that they would soon be arriving at Casselton. "Passengers leaving the train should make sure to take all of their baggage with them. Thank you for traveling with North Western Rail. We hope you have had a pleasant journey."

"All appearance is illusion," said Patrick. "The thing that does not change is the spirit, the essence of your being. That remains as God made it. Whatever shape, size, or form you have, there's *you* inside it, making it work."

The train drew into Casselton station. Patrick took two large cases from the rack above their heads and led the way out onto the platform. They looked impressive with flight labels stuck to the sides.

"Now," he said, "the first thing we must do is put these cases in the left luggage. We shall have no need of them."

"Then why did we bring them?" said Thomas.

"A precaution," said his father sheepishly. "Stella might have been puzzled if we had set out on a long journey without any luggage. We have two hours before the train to Edinburgh. I'll take you into Casselton and show you where I have really 'worked' these past five years. There is something there I need to collect."

"Edinburgh?" said Thomas. "I thought we were going to London."

"That was part of the story for Stella," said Patrick ruefully. "London would be no use to us at all. In Edinburgh is the castle on the hill. And the monument in the park. You will remember them."

Chapter 10

Walgate Hill

They came out of Casselton station, crossed the broad road outside its giant portico, turned left, right, and left again. Then they were at the foot of a steep hill with old buildings on either side and a busy road running down the middle.

Thomas clung to Patrick's sleeve, walking quickly to keep pace with his father's longer stride. This part of town seemed to him dirty, noisy, and much too crowded. They walked up on the left-hand side of the street, passing shoddy-looking shops with grimy windows. On the other side of the road were a betting shop, a post office, then a terrace of high houses with steep front gardens that seemed to frown down at all the passing traffic. Their elegance had clearly known better days.

"This is Walgate Hill," said Patrick. "Here is where I have worked for the past five years."

"Here!" said Thomas, surprised and by no means impressed. "I thought you worked at the Chemicals Complex. Stella thought you did."

The Chemicals Complex was part of an international company. It was the biggest and best employer in the area.

"A natural mistake," said Patrick. "I thought it better not to correct it."

Suddenly they were brought to a halt.

Patrick felt someone push quite roughly against his right shoulder and a voice shouted, "Who you pushin,' mister? Who d'you think you're shovin'?"

Thomas jumped, glad to be on his father's other side, wondering what would happen next.

Patrick, however, was not in the least startled. He knew the voice and he knew the speaker's way of joking. He laughed and turned to face his assailant.

"All right, Canty, me old son," he said. "Hold your horses! Hold your horses!"

The man was small and dark, his long, scruffy hair tied back in a ponytail. His overcoat, dull brown and threadbare, reached almost to his feet. His face was wizened and his smile gap-toothed. The dark eyes twinkled, though, as if there were always something to be happy about.

"Here," said Patrick, handing him some coins, "and don't say I'm not good to you!"

"Ye are, Mr. Bentley. Ye allus are!"

He peered behind Patrick at Thomas, who had retreated as far as possible. Canty could see his head peeping round cautiously, a dark little head with deep brown eyes. He could see the shiny green coat the boy was wearing and the tan-colored knitted woolen gloves.

"That your lad?" he said.

"Yes," said Patrick.

"Hello, Sammy," said the tramp. "You look like a Sammy to me. I'm nivver wrong about a name! I could make me livin' at it! I've often thought about settin' up in a booth on the town moor."

Thomas smiled nervously but said nothing. He was glad when they hurried on up the hill, leaving Canty to his own devices.

"Who was he?" he said when they were safely clear.

"Just a friend of mine," said Patrick. "I've known him ever since I came here."

"He's awful," said Thomas.

"No, he's not," said Patrick, shaking his head and smiling. "He's unfortunate and downtrodden. Life has not been kind to him, probably from the start. He's not the sort who would ever be sent on a mission to outer space. There is no risk of anyone like him landing on Ormingat. But he'll find his way to heaven all right."

"And why did he call you Mr. Bentley?"

"He makes up his own mind what people are called. My office is above Bentley's Cycle Store. That's where he first saw me. There was no point in correcting him. He wouldn't have taken any notice if I had."

Just then they came to a shop with clean windows and bicycles chained up on the pavement outside. *Bent-*

ley's Cycle Store was written above the shop front in white letters on a vivid blue background.

"This is it," said Patrick, leading the way to a door further up than the shop. He took a key from his pocket, opened the door, and took Thomas into a small lobby from which a flight of linoleum-clad wooden stairs led to the flat above.

"All the modern conveniences," said Patrick with a wry smile as they reached the landing. "Lavatory, washroom, kitchen—and my office, looking out onto the busiest, dirtiest street in Casselton."

Inside the office there was a large desk, totally bare and polished clean, an office chair, an old leather armchair, and not very much else.

"It wasn't quite as empty as this when I worked here," said Patrick. "I cleared everything out earlier this week. All I have to do now is pick up my case from the wall safe, do a final check, then lock up and put the keys in the post."

He didn't hurry to do all of this. There was time to spare and he wanted to make the picture clearer to his bewildered son. For five years he had avoided talking about his work in Casselton. Like many another father, when he came home he switched off that part of his life. Belthorp was a world away.

"Here's where I converted your notebooks into microfilm," he said. "I have every one of them ready to take home with us. Does that surprise you?"

Thomas considered this. He had never known where his notebooks went. He had always filled one and then was given another. It was so much part of the system that it had never occurred to him to question it.

"But where are the notebooks?" he said.

"I had to destroy them," said Patrick. "They were too bulky. You are quite a prolific writer!"

Thomas was not quite sure what *prolific* meant, but he let that pass.

"I have kept the very first one," said Patrick, "but that is for what you might call sentimental reasons."

Thomas went to the window to look down on the street. Patrick followed him and raised the sash so that they could look out more easily, resting their arms on the sill. The day was cold but crisp. Somewhere in the distance a clock told the hour with eleven clear strokes.

"This is something I have done many a time," said Patrick, turning his head to look up and down the hill. "I've written my own descriptions of this sad bit of the city, though it was not the chief part of the mission. Your work was more important."

Thomas had given up on asking why it was important, but Patrick decided to explain a little further.

"These Earth people are clever," he said. "One day they may discover Ormingat, though it might take centuries. When they arrive on our planet, we want to know how to communicate with them from the start. We want to understand everything about them. We want to know what it is like to *be* human at all stages of life."

"And they'll know all that from what I've written?" said Thomas, baffled. "The people who come could be

Chinese, Russian, or anything. Then what use would it be?"

"Your accounts are just a very small piece in the jigsaw. But you are rather special," said his father with a smile. "You are the youngest, the youngest ever. All over Earth, our spies—I suppose that's what we should call them—have for years and years been adding to our knowledge. There are Ormingatrig everywhere."

"So why have I never met any? Why do we not know any of them?"

Even as he asked his question, Thomas was diverted by all of the life going on below. For him, this was a totally new experience. In five years on Earth his visits outside the village had been to places of great beauty, as holiday treats. No one would come to Walgate Hill for a holiday!

Beneath the window someone ran down the pavement pushing an old hand-barrow and other pedestrians shouted at him indignantly to be more careful. At the top of the hill, on the other side of the road, a huge brewery tanker was feeding beer through thick concertina tubes into the cellar of a public house. Cars and buses went up and down. People of all ages, shapes, and sizes passed, English and Asian in about equal proportions. The area was poor but cosmopolitan.

"One of *our* people could be down there," said Patrick. "For all I know, I could have run into one at any time. We visitors to Earth are not permitted to know or communicate with one another. It is part of the Covenant."

61

"Why?" said Thomas. "And what's the Covenant?"

"It's a sort of agreement," said Patrick. "We are here to observe, not to conspire. We must never, ever pose a threat to Earth, or even seem to do so. You and I are here with a job to do. What others do is none of our business. We have no wish to colonize or to conquer. We are here simply to learn, and to be prepared in case Earth ever, God forbid, decides to invade us."

Thomas had learned in history about invasions. They were frightening.

"Would they?" he said. "Would they ever try to conquer Ormingat?"

"It's not something you or I need to worry about," said Patrick. "So far, they lack the ability. By the time they possess it, we can only hope that they will have become less aggressive. We, in our turn, will be ready to greet them as friends, in whatever language they speak. They may see us as aliens, but we shall know *them* through and through."

Patrick leaned on the sill with his hands clasped in front of him. For him too, the human life surrounding them was a distraction.

He looked at his hands pensively. Strong hands with short stubby fingers and square fingernails.

"Sometimes I forget that this is just a spacesuit, this body I inhabit," he said. "That's all it is, created from a culture of DNA to give me safe passage to, from, and about Earth. Yet now it feels like part of me. I shall be in some ways reluctant to shed it. It will be like losing an old friend."

He looked down at Thomas, who had adopted the

same stance by his father's side. The boy's hands, tapering fingers, clasped together, looked fine and frail.

"You too," said Patrick. "That body of yours is for Earth only and for the journey home. A better genetic match would have made us resemble one another more closely! On Ormingat you and I are unmistakably parent and child."

But at that very moment the resemblance was there in the wistful longing each of them felt—not a simple yearning to be human, something much more impossible than that: to be Earthling and Ormingatriga both at once. Thomas was beginning to picture more clearly what it would be like to be Tonitheen. The words of the Ormingat tongue were foreign to him, but the music was part of his being. Come home, Tonitheen. Agmalish, Argule, Ergay—

Patrick drew back from the window and closed it.

"Now," he said. "Time we were leaving. You sit in the armchair while I see to things."

Seeing to things meant first of all going to a little side cupboard with a long slim door. Inside was the wall safe. The case Patrick produced was in fact just a soft leather document case fastened by an all-round zip. Its sides bulged with knobbly contents, but the whole was not too big to go into the "poacher's pocket" in Patrick's sheepskin coat.

"The microfilms are in here," he explained to Thomas, "and one or two other things."

Next he took from a drawer in the desk a brand-new, sharp, and shiny garden trowel.

Thomas looked at him, puzzled.

63

"That's all right," said Patrick as he wrapped the trowel in a plastic bag and put it in the side pocket of the coat. "You never know when it might come in handy."

Thomas smiled warily but said nothing.

Finally Patrick sealed the keys up in a small padded envelope, already stamped. It was addressed to Morgan, Dace & Redford in accordance with some arrangement made before Patrick came to Casselton. He did not know who would receive the keys or what would happen to the office. That was none of his business.

"We'll just pop these in the post box as we go," he said.

Chapter 11

The Accident

The brewery tanker at the top of the hill had finished its delivery to the Bay Horse. The driver and his mate climbed into the high cabin, their next port of call the Blue Bell, on the other side of the river.

"Time d'you make it, Jack?" said the driver to his mate.

"Just after quarter to twelve. I'll not be sorry when *this* shift's over, Andy. I've got a head like a stairhead!"

Andy put the engine into gear and pressed lightly on the accelerator. Walgate Hill had to be taken very gently. The driver was only too well aware that his juggernaut was traveling down a busy road with the steepest gradient in town.

The tanker rolled away, the driver carefully grasping the steering wheel and soft-pedaling the brake. Suddenly the vehicle gathered speed and more speed. The driver pushed the brake down further, easily at first, properly, sensibly, but then with growing force as he realized that there was no response. Faster it went, faster and faster. Both men in the cab were in a state of panic as they realized that the brakes had failed completely.

"Hell!" shouted the driver. "Bloody hell!"

But before you think too badly of him, that was not what he was *thinking*. Thought moves fast, faster than sound, faster than light, faster than words, believe me. . . . *If the lights stay green, if I can get this monster across the junction, Lilly Street, Cromer Street, then steer a straight line into the old public lavatories in the middle of the road, no deaths, no serious damage, and maybe, dear God, we'll even live through it . . . this vehicle's tough as a tank . . . no, no, no, no, no, no. . . . Pelican Crossing! lights red, man and child, child running, envelope in hand, man walking, sheepskin coat, post office van far side of the lights . . . stopping . . . stopping! . . . move, move, move, ye beggar! move! . . . hazard lights, horn, horn, horn, damn these bloody brakes!*

Thoughts condensed, and even more of them than those listed, thoughts faster than words, faster than sound, faster than light, but totally, totally helpless.

The tanker crazed over the crossing, missing the child, hitting the man, and careening into the post office van, half swallowing it beneath colossal wheels.

Thomas ran and put the envelope in the letter box. And at that precise moment, behind him, came the loudest noise he had ever heard in his whole life. Sound and sound alone shook his body and threw him to the ground. Others on the pavement screamed. A woman with a stroller dived into the post office. Two girls huddled together beside the shop window. The first reaction of those nearest was to crouch and cower. Then, as the noise of the crash stopped, a wave of onlookers surged forward. Thomas would have been crushed had not one man noticed him, lifted him to his feet, and pushed him back out of the way.

Two or three cars had time to pass on the other side, going uphill. Then traffic was halted on that side too as a siren screamed. Policemen in a squad car came speeding down the hill, frantically summoned by a bystander on his mobile telephone. They hurried in to clear the way and to help prepare for the emergency services that would very soon follow.

One policeman moved people on while his colleague went first to the post office van, whose driver was slumped over the wheel. The back of the van was totally telescoped under the tanker. The policeman was able to reach into the front of the van, to ascertain that the driver was still alive, but heaven alone knew for how much longer.

The tanker itself was less damaged. The policeman climbed up on the step of the cab, saw its two occupants lurched forward, but was relieved to hear them groan and to see movements that suggested more possibility of life than in the van below.

"Can you manage to sit back?" said the policeman loudly. It seemed a sensible suggestion—it would help their breathing, show that that they were conscious. It was also something simple they could do, or not do, without thinking too much.

The driver heaved himself back on his seat by pushing on the steering wheel. He looked at the policeman in a dazed fashion and then said brokenly, "The man, the man . . ."

"He's trapped in his van," said the policeman. "He's not dead. The ambulance and the fire brigade are on their way. We can hope."

"The *man*," said the driver, "the man in the crossing."

His mate jerked back into his seat and gave a shriek of pain.

"Hold still," said the policeman, hoping that his earlier suggestion had been the right one. "Help'll be here any minute."

"But the man on the crossing, the man in the sheepskin coat," said the driver again. It cost him an effort to speak; his face was ashen with pain; but it was something he had to say.

This time the policeman realized what the driver must mean. He jumped down from the step and looked anxiously at the front of the cab, at the high wheels that in themselves were a colossal weight, the thick mudguards, and to the front of them the mangled rear end of the post office van all entangled so that only the brigade with cutting gear would be able to prize them apart. A man? In *there*?

There was no sign of anybody.

68

The policeman jumped up on the step again.

"There's nobody there," he said.

"There has to be," said the driver as he became more coherent. "I ran him over, God help him. He must be under the wheels."

Other police cars arrived on the scene, a medic on a motorbike, then a fire engine. Watchers were herded further down the street, where a cluster of them waited outside the betting shop, determined to see everything.

It was then that one of the firemen noticed the boy sitting on the pavement in front of the post office window, his knees drawn up to his chin.

"Come on, young'un," said the fireman. "We'll have to have you away from there. Are you all right?"

Thomas did not even look at him. He was shivering convulsively.

"Hey," said the fireman, lifting him into his arms, "nasty shock you've had, but you'll be all right. Don't worry. We'll see to you, get you back to your mam. What's your name, old son? Mine's Steve."

Then he looked down the street toward the group of spectators.

"Anyone know this bairn?"

He walked with him toward the crowd.

"It's Sammy," said a voice. "It's Sammy Bentley."

Canty pushed his way to the front of the group. He had recognized the boy's clothing first, but now he saw clearly that there was no mistaking him—his dark, straight hair and fine features showed distinctively the face Canty had first seen earlier that day.

"And how do you know him?" said the fireman, looking doubtfully at the scruffy little vagrant.

"Know his dad," said Canty. "Saw'm with his dad the smornin'. You ask 'im. 'E'll tell yis."

Thomas lay in the fireman's arms like a baby. He did not look at Canty. He looked at nobody. The fireman stood waiting, wondering what to do next.

"Well, who's his dad, Canty?" said one of the policemen, recognizing him from previous encounters.

"Mr. Bentley, sir," said Canty respectfully. It always pays to respect the law.

"And who's Mr. Bentley?" said the policeman patiently.

"Mr. Bentley's . . . Mr. Bentley," said Canty, not knowing what else to say. "You must have seen him. Comes up here most days. Well dressed. Canny fella. Allus a kind word."

"What was he wearing this morning?" asked the policeman who had been first on the scene. He had a sickening feeling that he knew what the answer would be.

"One of them sheepskin coats," said Canty.

Just then the first ambulance arrived.

The policeman turned urgently to the fireman who was holding Thomas.

"Take the boy to the ambulance," he said. "Sooner he's out of here the better."

After Thomas was safely in the ambulance, the policeman turned to the others and said quietly, "I hope I'm wrong, but from what the driver said, I think Mr. Bentley might be crushed in the wreckage."

But when the emergency services had done all they could, and a crane and a cutter had been brought to disentangle the wreckage, no body was found, not a sign anywhere of the man in the sheepskin coat.

There was one strange bit of evidence. Embedded in the tire of the near-side front wheel was a torn strip of sheepskin, two inches wide and about eighteen inches long.

Chapter 12

In the Hospital

There were four admissions to Casselton General Hospital as a result of the crash on Walgate Hill. Four beds were newly occupied just as the staff was trying to get as many patients as possible home for Christmas. That's the way it goes.

Chris Patel, the driver of the post office van, sustained the worst injuries. He was taken straight into intensive care and prepared for any surgery he might need, but it looked as if he would live through the horror of the crash. He would survive because he was slightly built and cantankerous. A bigger man might well have perished. A less volatile one might not have had such a will to live.

Andy Brown, the tanker driver, and his mate, Jack Jordan, were in the men's ward on the top floor, being treated for shock, abrasions, and fractured limbs. And they still insisted, both of them, that the tanker had somehow crushed a man in a sheepskin coat. On that story police could not budge them, even though all the evidence was against it.

In the nearly empty children's ward, Sammy Bentley, or whatever his real name might turn out to be, was put in a bed next to a very talkative boy about his own age who was due to go home next day.

"Sammy hasn't uttered a word since he was picked up," said the doctor, looking at the notes. "We've done all the usual tests. We can't find anything physically wrong with him. What's more, he has accepted food and drink when it's been put in front of him. He walks as far as he needs. But then there is that total silence. His eyes won't even look at you. Putting him beside Jamie might help. Kids react to kids."

"He might prefer peace and quiet," said the male nurse, with an expression that was comically doubtful. "Jamie is a bit overpowering."

"Jamie's racket might just do the trick," said the doctor, smiling. "It might bring the boy out of himself. And if it doesn't, it certainly won't do Jamie any harm! Besides, the Demon of the North goes home tomorrow. We'll all have peace and quiet after that!"

"Won't we just!" said the nurse with a grin.

It was after teatime when Thomas was finally put to bed in a pair of hospital pajamas. The curtain was drawn round his bed. The nurse folded his clothes and put them into his locker. Nothing was to be done that might make the boy feel more insecure.

In the next bed, the infamous Jamie was sitting up nursing a portable electronic keyboard, a "poorly present" from his mam and dad. He had set it on auto and it kept on playing "When the Saints Go Marching In" over and over again.

"Give it a rest, James," said the male nurse. "The saints must be tired of marching by now!"

"You'll not hear it after tomorrow, Ernie," said Jamie with a friendly smile that might or might not have been cheeky. Blond children always look so innocent! "I'm taking it home with me."

"I know," said the nurse. "And I'm going to do a dance on the roof when it's gone! But for now, we've brought you a new pal. His name's Sammy."

"Through there?" said Jamie, nodding toward the curtain.

"Yes," said the nurse quietly. "Talk to him, Jamie, there's a good lad. He's had a bit of a fright."

"Is that why he's here?" said Jamie, puzzled. Surely people didn't go to the hospital because they'd had a fright.

"Let him tell you himself," said the nurse. "Talk to him, but don't ask him any questions. Wait till he talks back to you. That way you'll be helping him. You'll even be helping me—and Dr. Ramsay! In fact, he specially asked for you to do it. So remember, plenty of talk, no questions."

Jamie was visibly flattered.

The nurse had been sitting close to Jamie's bed, talking in a low voice. Now he stood up and drew aside the curtain to reveal the boy in question propped up on pillows in the next bed.

"This is Sammy," he said. "Sammy, this is Jamie.

Make the most of him today—he's off home tomorrow. I'll leave you to get to know one another."

Jamie leaned over toward Thomas's bed. The hospital was boring and Jamie was eager to talk to anybody. And it did sound as if Sammy might be interesting to know. Fancy being in the hospital because you got a fright! It would be worth hearing about.

"Hello, Sammy," he said enthusiastically. "They call me Jamie Martin."

The boy in the next bed looked straight ahead and ignored this friendly overture.

"I've had me 'pendix out," said Jamie, thinking that might be interesting, and hoping for another story in exchange for his own. "It's been trying to get out for ages. I used to have a grumbling 'pendix. Me dad said he didn't know what a 'pendix should have to grumble about, but we're glad it's gone."

Jamie paused to allow the other boy to chip in. But Thomas did not even look his way.

"I'm going home tomorrow," said Jamie, "but I've got to come back for a checkup after Christmas. I had a really bad 'pendix, far worse than the ordnerry sort."

That information produced no response.

"I'm getting a bike for Christmas," said Jamie, deciding that maybe his appendix operation was not interesting enough, "and some computer games—don't know what they are, it's supposed to be a surprise."

Thomas went on staring straight in front of him and said nothing.

Jamie tried another tack, thinking the boy in the next bed might be miserable at being in the hospital.

75

"They'll let you out for Christmas, you know," he said. "They try to let everybody out for Christmas. And at least you're not on a drip. I was on a drip. They stuck a needle right in me arm and it was fixed to a tube goin' up a to a bottle on a frame. It was really awkward when I had to go to the you-know-where. Me and me frame with the bottle gettin' along the ward and into the bathroom! It was on wheels but it wasn't easy to steer."

The boy in the next bed still did not look his way. The expression on his face remained wooden. "Awkward when I had to go to the you-know-where" should at least have raised a smile!

"Me drip came out once," said Jamie, trying harder to make a joke of it, "and the nurse—he's called Ernie—was hopping mad and really jumping up and down, but he was just kidding. I think."

Jamie paused and then said anxiously, "*You* haven't got a rucktured 'pendix. *You* won't be on a drip."

This last remark was added for comfort. It wouldn't do to frighten the boy even more, especially if he was a nervous type. Jamie was beginning to be worried at his neighbor's lack of attention.

"You can hear me, can't you?" he said.

Thomas *could* have been deaf. He showed no sign of having heard anything.

"I once had an *elephant* called Sammy," said Jamie in desperation. "It was made of gray velvet and had red ears—red on the inside, gray on the out. It's still in my cupboard. They wanted to give it to me little brother,

but he would only have chewed it. He chews everything."

Even this met with stony silence. There is only so
much a boy can take. Jamie was peeved. It occurred to
him that Sammy was playing dumb on purpose.

"All right," he said, pulling his sheets up to his chin.
"Be like that! I didn't ask you to come here. Nurse!
Nurse!"

A nurse's aide who was passing came hurrying over.
She had just come onto the ward for the evening shift,
had not even had time to see the head nurse yet, and
here was her "favorite" patient already demanding attention.

"What is it, Jamie?" she said. "What is it this time?"

"I don't like *him*," said Jamie glowering at Thomas.
"He won't even look at me. And I haven't asked him
any questions. I did just what Ernie said I should do. I
want to move to that bed over there."

He pointed to an empty bed in the corner of the
ward furthest away from his own. In high-sided cots to
one side of it, two young children were already
sleeping.

"Sammy's not doing you any harm," said the aide,
glancing down at the name on the clipboard at the
foot of the new patient's bed. "I can't move you without permission, Jamie, and I probably wouldn't get it
anyway. You're going home tomorrow. Why don't you
just ignore him if he's ignoring you? That would seem
to be the best plan."

"Well, put the telly on," said the boy sulkily. "I want

to watch the telly. Anything's better than looking at that dummy."

"All right, Jamie," said the aide. "You can both watch telly. That mightn't be a bad idea."

She turned to the other bed.

"You'd like to watch telly, wouldn't you, Sammy? I think there's a comedy program coming on."

Thomas did not flicker an eyelid. The young nurse was worried. She raised his wrist and took his pulse. Then she adjusted the television for Jamie and went back to report what she thought an alarming condition in the new patient.

"His pulse is normal," she said, "but he is totally unresponsive. When I let go of his wrist, it just dropped like a dead weight."

"We know that, Cornelia," said the head nurse. "We've been told just to monitor, not to do anything else for the moment. Let me or Ernie know straight-away if you see any sign of change."

Jamie set his keyboard going again, in competition with the television. Then he lay back on his pillows and fell asleep, as if lulled by all the noise.

The young nurse's aide crept up quietly, removed the keyboard, and restored the peace. When Jamie's mother and aunt came in to see him half an hour later he was lying there like a cherub, and they both looked at him lovingly and forgot what a terror he would be when they took him home.

"I think we'll just go," they whispered to the aide after they had both sat in silence for ten minutes. "It seems a shame to disturb him. He looks so peaceful. And he'll be home in his own bed tomorrow."

From time to time they had glanced across at the other bed. The little boy lying there with his dark eyes wide open, staring in front of him, was disconcerting. Neither of the visitors spoke to him, but each felt relieved to move away.

"Is the boy in the bed next to our Jamie *all right*?" said Jamie's mother as they passed the desk on their way out. She was clearly worried that her son might have been placed alongside some juvenile psychopath.

The male nurse at the desk looked up at her and smiled.

"He's had a shock, that's all," he said. "We're keeping an eye on him. A good night's sleep should make all the difference. *He*'ll probably be going out tomorrow as well."

The women looked back at the boy quite kindly now. They would have stayed to hear more about the shock. But Ernie deliberately looked down at the papers on the desk and did not raise his head till they had left.

After they had gone, he went over to Thomas's bed and drew the curtain round it. It was a shame, he thought, that no one had thought of doing that before the visitors arrived. Ernie settled the patient down, removing the extra pillows to make him more comfortable. He smiled at Thomas as he did so and said a very quiet goodnight. But there was no acknowledgment.

"Suit yourself, young Sam," said Ernie. "See you in the morning."

In the middle of the night, when the lights in the ward were dimmed, Thomas muttered into his pillow his first words since the crash: "*Vateelin, Vateelin mesht . . .*" and began very quietly to weep.

Chapter 13

Investigations Under Way

"We have carried out a thorough autopsy on the visible remains of your deceased specimen of *Ovis aries*. Our findings would indicate that it is of considerable age, for the species, but in a state of preservation suggesting that care and attention and tanning have gone into the process," said Bill from the lab with a perfectly straight face and his customary plethora of circumlocutions.

He returned the plastic bag containing the strip of sheepskin to Sergeant Morland, whose job it was to collate and pass on all information.

"What is more," Bill continued, "there is nothing to suggest that any drop of human blood or fragment of human bone is embedded in the fiber. What made your inspector think there might be? We didn't even find a flea. To put it succinctly, it's just a bit of old coat."

"How did it get to be 'a bit'?" said the sergeant.

"Was it ripped, cut, or torn? How do you think it happened?"

"Now there," said Bill, "we *can* help you. The tear was recent and had probably been caused by sudden, violent friction against a piece of red-painted metal. The paint exactly matches the paint on the post office van. There is also some rust matching that on the inner rims of the tanker's mudguards. This would suggest that the coat from which the piece comes had somehow been nipped between the tanker and the van at the moment of collision. The torn piece then adhered to the tanker's front wheel and was spun round with it."

"Very good," said Sergeant Morland dryly. "Spectacular. But where then is the rest of the coat?"

"That's not our worry," said Bill. "That's a problem for the police! Anyway, the written report will be with you in the morning. But Inspector Galway wanted to know quickly what it would contain. I reckon what we *have* done is pretty spectacular. We got this material at five o'clock and here I am with the answers and it's just turned nine. My job's done, and so will yours be once you've passed the buck!"

The whole business was becoming more and more complicated by the minute. It should have been simple: a runaway vehicle, a crash, people in the hospital, vehicles towed away for inspection, faults found, cause confirmed, and then it would be up to the law to sort out blame and award compensation. But no, not this one. The crash, at the most inconvenient time of the year, just before the holiday, had to be different. Two men in hospital were swearing blind they'd run someone over. And a boy, struck dumb by the event, was in the same hospital, unclaimed and not very clearly identified.

"Now, Canty," said Sergeant Morland when he had tracked down the vagrant to an alleyway between Walgate Hill and Mercer Street, "I'd like you to come to the station with me. There'll be a nice cup of tea for you there, and we might even have some chocolate tea cakes." This was inducement enough on a cold winter's night, not to mention the importance of being driven there in a police car.

"Take your time," said the sergeant when he had his guest sitting comfortably in the "better class" interview room. "Who is Mr. Bentley? What do you know about him?"

"He's well-off," said Canty, "but not posh, at least not stuck-up."

"What does he do?" said the sergeant. "What's his job?"

"I wouldn't know *that*!" said Canty impatiently. "How d'ye think I'd know *that*? He nivver wears a uniform."

"Is there anything, any single thing, you can tell us about him? We'd be very pleased you know. It would make our job a lot easier. Do you know his first name?"

Canty brightened. His little coaly eyes gleamed and he smiled his gap-toothed smile.

"Ye shud've asked us afore!" he said. "His first name's Todd. I'm sure it is. Todd Bentley."

83

The sergeant was not totally convinced.

"It has a ring to it," he said. "Todd Bentley. Yes. But how do you know?"

"I know," said Canty. "I can't rightly remember how I know. But I do. I suppose he might be some relation to the old fella in the bike shop. I've seen him near there a few times."

The shop was closed, of course. It was turned ten o'clock at night. Sergeant Morland was still on duty, still collating information and asking questions on the telephone. He found out where the shop owner lived and was glad of an excuse to get away from his desk. A squad car gave him a lift to Parkfield Road. It was at the other end of town, the good end with the semidetached houses and the neat front gardens.

"Mr. Bentley?" said Sergeant Morland to the gray-haired man who answered the door. The dog by the man's side growled quietly.

"Yes?" said the man, looking wary.

"Police," said Sergeant Morland. "We are trying to trace a Mr. Todd Bentley and we wondered if you could help us in any way."

The man opened the door wider; the dog relaxed. Somewhere in the background a voice was calling, "Who is it? Is that our Jill?"

"No, Pamela," said the man over his shoulder. "It's nothing. Just a policeman looking for somebody called Todd Bentley."

The shop owner turned to the sergeant again and

said, "I'm afraid you've got the wrong Bentley. Never heard of anybody called Todd."

"It was a long shot," said Sergeant Morland. "I thought Canty might be mistaken."

"Canty!" said the real Mr. Bentley with a laugh. "You can't take Canty's word for anything! He's harmless enough, but he makes it all up as he goes along. Who's this fella you're looking for?"

Sergeant Morland explained briefly that a boy had been picked up in a state of shock after the accident (no need to tell about the accident—everyone who had been on Walgate Hill at the time knew what had happened, more or less).

"His name might be Sammy Bentley," said the sergeant, "but we do have only Canty's word for it. What is true is that there is a child in the hospital who's in some sort of shock and refusing to speak."

"It's a wonder nobody's looking for him," said Gerald Bentley.

Sergeant Morland smiled wearily.

"I just wish somebody would!" he said.

"So," said Inspector Galway as he looked down quite lovingly at the piece of sheepskin, "what have we got?"

"Do you really want to know, sir?" said the sergeant, stifling a yawn. It was after midnight. Morland knew that if it hadn't been for the confounded piece of sheepskin, both he and his inspector would have been home by now. There was something about this business that appealed to Inspector Galway. He just loved a mystery, and there weren't enough of them to go round. The crimes he met with, even the nastiest, were mostly anything but mysterious. Now he looked sharply at his sergeant, irritated at being stopped in his tracks.

"Well?" he said.

"We've got precisely nothing," said Morland doggedly. "If those two men in the hospital would stop hallucinating and if that boy would open his mouth and talk, we would be a lot better off. As it is, we might as well go home and sleep on it. And, by the way, your wife rang up an hour ago saying that the cats enjoyed your supper."

Inspector Galway smiled. He got on well with Morland. It was not the first time such a message had been passed on. It would not be the last.

Galway looked down thoughtfully at the tantalizing piece of sheepskin.

"You do realize, Morland," he said, "that this is quite a remarkable mystery? It could almost be an encounter with the supernatural!"

Chapter 14

Night Thoughts

Cornelia heard the sobbing, low though it was. She went quietly to the bed in the corner and leaned over Thomas's pillow, stroking his head gently.

"There, there, Sammy," she said. "Try to sleep, love. You'll feel better in the morning."

Thomas ceased his sobbing and listened carefully to the soft voice.

"If you want anything, I won't be far away," said the nurse, cautious of saying more because of the business of "monitoring." Recalling the thing that most embarrassed a child in hospital, she added, "There's slippers in your locker and the bathroom's just at the end of the ward if you need it. Or I can bring you a bottle if you'd rather."

Thomas shrugged to show he had heard this vital bit of information. He had already been taken to the bathroom, but he had been wondering a bit anxiously whether he could just get up and go there in what seemed like the middle of the night.

"I think Sammy's coming out of it," Cornelia said to the head nurse when she went over to the desk. "There's a definite change. He's having a bit of a weep, but he didn't seem to want anything."

At that moment, a little boy in hospital foam slippers padded to the end of the ward, in the direction of the bathroom. Cornelia looked round, startled, and saw it was Sammy. The head nurse put a finger to her lips but indicated that Cornelia should follow him discreetly. He went in. He came out. And he returned to his bed like a sleepwalker.

"It's a start," said the head nurse. "We should be able to get him talking tomorrow."

In bed once more, Thomas lay on his back gazing up at the ceiling. But he was not in a state of shock any longer. His faculties had fully returned to him. He was silently, furiously thinking.

First of all, he took in fully his present situation. *This is a hospital bed. That is a curtain. Beyond that curtain is another bed. In that bed there is . . .* He struggled. *There is a boy called Jamie who talks.* That was as much of the present and of the near past as Thomas could gather into his fuddled brain.

He tried hard to remember the time before he arrived in the hospital bed, but there was a great gap in his memory. He could not fathom how he had arrived at this place and time.

The last thing he could genuinely remember was putting an envelope into a post box. It was late morning. His father was walking behind him, crossing the road. Then the crash! The noise! And the being totally alone . . .

Thomas had a surge of resentment.

Why had his father left him there? *Where* was Patrick? He had promised no harm would come to his son. Was this not harm? To be left all alone in a strange place?

Thoughts took puzzling leaps . . . The nurse had called him Sammy. That was the name the tramp had given him. Did the people in this town always call strangers "Sammy"? What should he do about telling them his real name?

My real name is not even Thomas. My real, real name is Tonitheen, he thought, *and I come from Ormingat.* Names never uttered except to his father when they were alone, names he had been trained never to tell to anyone else on Earth. For the first time in his life, he was fully aware of his true origins. To know the words—and he had always known the words—was one thing, to face the facts was quite another.

Thomas heard footsteps and saw the curtain move. It was the nurse coming quietly to check her patient. Thomas shut his eyes and let his head fall to one side to make it look as if he were sleeping. Cornelia looked in on him briefly, was satisfied, and went away.

Thomas, left to his thoughts again, bit his sheet so that he would not begin to sob. The thoughts were so sad and so terrible. *Where are you, Vateelin mesht? The*

crash must have something to do with it. The crash . . .
Oh, Father, can it be that you are dead?

No, thought Thomas with determination, *he is* not
dead. If he were dead, I would know. I would somehow be
bound to know.

He has gone in search of the spaceship. He has gone and
left me here. He must have had some strong reason but clearly
I am not as important as the assignment he is meant to keep.
If he really loved me, he would be here by my bed.

Then, into the vacuum left by this idea, there crept a
treacherous thought.

I know where Stella is.

If I tell the people here that I am Thomas Derwent and I
live in Belthorp, and give them Stella's name, they will send
for her and she will take me home.

It was a great temptation.

But my name is Tonitheen and I come from Ormingat and
Vateelin is my father. The names are keys. Patrick had said
the names were keys, to be used only in the direst of
circumstances. And there could surely be no circum-
stance more dire than this!

He did not tell me enough, thought Thomas angrily. *He*
did not trust me enough to explain it all. I do not know how
to use these keys. If he had wanted me to be prepared, he
should have told me more.

I can go home to Belthorp with Stella and spend Christmas
there and see my friends again. There need be no diminish-
ing, no terrifying journey. I can go on living here on Earth
and never worry about any of that.

More thoughts drifted in. . . .

They'll want to know where my father is. Stella will want to know. Everyone will want to know. Parents lose children sometimes. I've seen it on the news; parents do lose children. Then people hunt for them. But I have never known a child to lose a parent, not just in the middle of a street the way I did. And if I tell them everything, *that might be worse.*

I'll just have to say I do not know where my father is. The truth is always best. I was with him on Walgate Hill. Then there was a crash. And I have not seen him since.

If the truth is best, said a voice in his head like a prickly conscience, *then in this, the direst of circumstances, you know the truth, Tonitheen. You know what your father would expect you to do. Use the keys. To do anything else is an act of disloyalty. To do anything else solves nothing.*

How can words be keys? How can such keys work? Where are the locks?

Then Thomas remembered *abracadabra* and *open sesame.* They were just words uttered into the air and working magic. In stories! In childish fairy stories!

But Patrick had said that the spaceship was not magic. It was all science—diminishing, increasing, black holes, and energy—so neither would the key words be magic. They too must be science. *And if the only thing I know how to do is to say them, then that is what I must do.*

Say them, said the voice inside his head. *Say them out loud and clearly.*

 It was three o'clock in the morning. In the ward, other children were sleeping and a nurse and two

91

aides were watchful as they quietly carried out small tasks, checking and tidying.

The peace was shattered when Thomas sat up straight in his bed and called out loudly, "I am Tonitheeen and I come from Ormingat!"

The voice was the voice of Ormingat. Its tone was high and thin, piercing the silence of the night and sounding like no accent on this Earth. The English words came out distorted by the alien voice.

Cornelia heard it with a shiver and rushed to the spot from which it appeared to come: Sammy's bed, in the left-hand corner.

A child at the other side of the nearly empty ward heard it and began to cry loudly. The other nurse's aide rushed to pacify him.

Jamie heard strange noises and turned over in his sleep.

Cornelia gripped Thomas by the shoulders.

"What are you doing, Sammy?" she said in a loud whisper. "I've never heard anything like it! How are you making that sound?"

It flashed through her mind that somehow Sammy might have produced this exotic noise on Jamie's keyboard, though Jamie himself had never managed anything quite so weird.

Thomas looked directly at her, making her instantly aware that he had left behind his zombie state of the evening before.

"I am Tonitheen," he said once more. "And I come from Ormingat."

The voice was the same, so out of keeping with any

voice the nurse had ever heard that she could not understand any of the words. The head nurse came over and stood behind her.

"I think we'd better call Dr. Wallace," said the head nurse. "This makes no sense to me at all."

Thomas lay back disconsolate. The keys were obviously not working. Nothing had happened. He did not know what to do next. *What you have to consider,* said the voice inside his head, *is what not to say. You have declared for Ormingat. Let your declaration stand firm.*

So when Dr. Wallace arrived, almost stumbling for lack of sleep, Thomas just looked at him and said nothing.

"What's wrong?" said the doctor, looking down at the notes that hung at the foot of the bed.

"He's spoken," said Nurse West primly. "At least, he's sort of spoken. We were told to let you know when any change occurred."

The young doctor stifled a yawn, listened to the patient's chest, and checked his pulse.

"Nothing odd there," he said. "What has he been saying?"

Cornelia and the head nurse looked at one another dubiously.

Thomas, seeing their difficulty, decided to help and said more softly this time, but in the same tones as before, "I am Tonitheen and I come from Ormingat."

Dr. Wallace heard and was suitably startled. He stared at Thomas openmouthed before looking down self-consciously at his notes. His experience of children on any but a clinical basis was very limited. He did not entirely trust them, and this one had just produced a sound that was mysteriously over the edge. To ask questions about it might expose him to ridicule.

Thomas smiled slightly, understanding perfectly well the doctor's dilemma. Using his Ormingat voice had turned into a game. All the worry was still there and all the distress, but to play was somehow to enlist on the side of optimism. Or, to put it more simply, he was an eleven-year-old boy with a healthy sense of fun that was as good a weapon as any against fear. If you can make a monkey out of people, you are not going to find them awesome!

"I see he is Dr. Ramsay's patient," said the doctor thoughtfully and with some relief. "There's nothing here that can't wait till morning. Dr. Ramsay will see him then."

Chapter 15

Saturday Morning

Next morning a different nurse came and drew back the curtain round Thomas's bed. It was then that he noticed for the first time that the ward was all decorated for Christmas. There were streamers hanging from the ceiling, looped between hoops that were garlanded with holly, mistletoe, and gold and silver tinsel. Whole bunches of balloons were tied to the tops of pillars that formed part of the wall between the ward and the corridor. Everything was sensibly out of reach.

"Breakfast, Sammy?" said the new nurse's aide. "I am Kirsty, here at your service. Would you like porridge or flakes? Not a bad hotel, this, even a choice of cereal!"

Kirsty chattered on. She had seen the notes and knew the problem. She was also hoping to hear this strange voice the others were talking about.

"Fell-akeses, plasselweese," said Thomas, pointing to

the bowl of cornflakes. The accent was real enough, but the words were invented, an eccentric, impromptu variation on "Flakes, please." Thomas enjoyed the expression on the aide's face. Surprise was soon followed by a look of comic disbelief. Kirsty was Scottish, down-to-earth, and not easily fazed. She put the tray across his lap and placed the bowl and spoon on it.

"Well, you're no' frae Glasgow," she said in an exaggerated Scottish accent, "and that's for sure."

Thomas smiled at her. And in his mind he was saying to himself, *I can like this game. It can last till it's all sorted out.*

"So," continued Kirsty, "is your name Sammy, or is it no'?"

"I am Tonitheen and I come from Ormingat."

Kirsty could not understand a word.

"That's harder than broad Geordie!" she said. "Let's look at your gums. Have you got some sort o' swazzle in there?"

Thomas very nearly spoke in his ordinary English voice. What on earth was a swazzle?

The aide held his chin between her thumb and forefinger and told him to open his mouth. He was so surprised that he did as he was told.

"No swazzle," said Kirsty, smiling. Thomas found it impossible to be vexed with someone whose smile was so jolly. Still, she shouldn't have looked in his mouth like that. He took a big spoonful of cornflakes before she could do it again.

In the next bed, Jamie had been listening wide-eyed to Thomas's amazing feats of alien sound.

"That's great!" he said when the aide moved away. "How do you do it?"

Thomas gave him a friendly grin and said, "I am Tonitheen and I come from Ormingat."

"Say that again," said Jamie enthusiastically.

"I am Tonitheen and I come from Ormingat," said Thomas in a louder voice.

Jamie listened as Thomas repeated the sentence three more times. Then he gave him a look of triumph.

"I yem Jameth Marriteen int I comf rom Cass-ell-tónn!" he shouted, so that the others in the ward all looked at him.

Kirsty came straight over to his bed.

"Do behave yourself, Jamie," she said. "There are two very poorly children over there—and you are going home as soon as the doctor's seen you, and your mam comes in."

"I was only trying to talk like Tobatheem," Jamie grumbled.

"Who?" said the aide.

"Him in the next bed," said Jamie impatiently. "His name's not Sammy, you know. It's Tobatheem. He's not English. I think he's African. Though he doesn't look it."

"Oh!" said Kirsty. "And here's me thinking he might be Irish. He sounds like a banshee to me! What makes you think he's from Africa?"

Jamie looked important. He was surely going to be asked to act as an interpreter!

"He comes from a place called Organmatt," said Jamie with the voice of authority. "And that is in Af-

97

rica, I think. I'm sure we learned about it in geography once."

Thomas nodded vigorously. This was even better!

"I am Tonitheen and I come from Ormingat."

"There, you see?" said Jamie. "It's easy to understand if you listen properly."

He returned Thomas's nods with interest and said, "I yem Jameth Marriteen int I comf rom Cass-ell-tónn!"

Then both boys laughed so that their bowls and spoons bounced on their trays.

"Now behave yourself, Jamie," said Kirsty, "and you too, whatever your name is! The doctor will be round in half an hour. Get on with your breakfast. Remember those poor children over there. Make less noise, the pair of you."

Thomas found it desperately difficult not to tell Jamie all about Belthorp Primary and his friend Mickey Trent. But he had made up his mind on a course of action and he was determined to stick to it. It was a bit like being a prisoner of war. He would tell only his name and number or, in his case, his own name and the name of the planet he had left at the age of three and did not even vaguely remember. Inventing fresh words would be dicey—Jamie seemed a bit too clever. So Thomas decided to stick to the original formula. Besides, his father somewhere, somehow, would be bound to hear him—the more he thought about it, the more he knew that must be true—and gibberish would hardly help. It was important not to lose sight of the real purpose of using the Ormingat tongue, the little he knew of it.

98

"I am Tonitheen and I come from Ormingat," said Thomas to his newfound friend.

"I yem Jameth Marriteen int I comf rom Cass-ell-tónn!" Jamie chanted in reply, and at the same time he set his keyboard to playing "Blaydon Races." It was quite noisy!

Then the head nurse came and drew the curtains round Jamie's bed.

"You can get ready to go home now," she said. "Dr. Ramsay will be along shortly, but I can't see there being any problems. It's away with you as soon as your mam arrives."

"I am Tonitheen," said Thomas through the curtain.

"I yem Jameth," Jamie called back to him.

Dr. Ramsay, Jamie's mother, and Ernie arrived together. The curtain was drawn back to show Jamie standing dressed and ready to go. Dr. Ramsay gave him a cursory glance and said, "Well, nothing to stop you going home, young man. See you next week. Your mother will make the appointment. If you would just call at reception before you go, Mrs. Martin . . ."

"Don't forget your instrument of torture, James," said Ernie, holding up the keyboard.

Jamie took the toy and thrust it down inside his sports bag.

"You feeling any better?" said Jamie's mother, looking benignly at Thomas. "You certainly look better than you did yesterday!"

"I am Tonitheen and I come from Ormingat," said Thomas loudly, and all who had not heard it before jumped and stared.

Ernie ran his fingers through his hair and said, "Not another one!"

Jamie's mother took her son by the hand and said quickly, "Time we were going now. Your dad's outside with the car."

Jamie turned to wave to Thomas, but Mrs. Martin pushed him on toward the exit.

⭐ "Well now, Sammy," said Dr. Ramsay, "I've had some odd reports about you. And that sound you just made is not what we expect from a sensible boy in a nice quiet hospital. So what's it all about, eh?"

"I am Tonitheen," said Thomas, "and I come from Ormingat."

Dr. Ramsay gave him a searching look and smiled slightly as he read in the notes of Kirsty Mackenzie's attempt to find the swazzle.

"What on earth is a swazzle?" he said.

"It's a thing used by Punch-and-Judy men, Dr. Ramsay," said Kirsty. "I thought Sammy might be using something of the kind to change his voice."

"It must be a talent," said Dr. Ramsay quite seriously. Then he turned to Thomas and said, "I'll be back to see you later, son. By then you may have decided to speak to me in plain English. I'm not much good at any other language."

Chapter 16

What Happened to Patrick?

What happened to Patrick was astonishing by any human reckoning.

It might sound like a feat of magic or even a miracle but it definitely wasn't. It was simply the sort of science that we don't know about. Ormingat science—gone wrong, as luck would have it.

In the split second after the tanker hit the van on Walgate Hill, the one pedestrian who should have been crushed between the two vehicles experienced a shock so great that he knew nothing for the next few hours.

But he did not die.

The lower edge of Patrick's sheepskin coat was caught and clamped in the clash of metal as if between the teeth of some fierce beast. The rest of him, like a lord a-leaping, flew through the air, his trajectory making a huge parabola that flung him to the other side of the road and onto the bonnet of a blue Mercedes that was speeding up the hill.

Its driver must have been aware of the crash, even if he saw it only through his mirror. He must have heard the noise of it. But, like many a non-Samaritan, he went on by. There would be plenty of witnesses on the other side of the road without his having to stop and waste time. So thought the driver behind him and the driver in front. They chose, quite sensibly, to see nothing.

And nobody saw Patrick?

Of course nobody saw Patrick.

In that tremendous, traumatic moment, he had mercifully diminished. The minuscule space he occupied on the blue car's bonnet was near the window trim, just below the hub that held the windscreen wiper. To the car's driver, he was completely invisible.

It is no good trying to explain or describe his size. The cosmic illusion, put under so severe a strain, had broken down. The man on the car bonnet was simply out of context, shrunk so much smaller than the normal things of Earth.

Fortunately, he knew nothing of this yet. He lay unconscious and inwardly healing as the car went westward up the hill and then turned north to join the traffic on the Great North Road.

 Vateelin's first thought as he regained a blurred consciousness was of his son.

"Tonitheen," he murmured. *"Tonitheen ban, mellissis enerf. Enin mellissis, Tonitheen ban."*

The blue car was traveling along the dual carriageway in growing darkness, on into the stretch of countryside where no lamps alleviated the gloom and stray animals diced with death. Vateelin raised himself on one elbow, then almost immediately collapsed again, settling in the angle of the windscreen wiper. The early evening was cold but dry.

When he woke up again, the car had stopped. Vateelin was aware that something had changed—motion to stillness, sound to silence have their own way of sending a message to the brain, bypassing consciousness.

Vateelin grasped the nearest handgrip, part of the mechanism that held the wiper's blade. He struggled round into a sitting position, then gazed about him, trying to make sense of his location.

His eyes first focused on himself, of course, his own body, his own clothes. The hem of his coat was torn ragged. The knuckles of his hands were scraped. His face felt sore, as if he had been punched. From his pocket he took his handkerchief and wiped his mouth. Even that was painful. His lips were bruised and swollen.

A wider exploration revealed a something he was clinging to, something too close to be identified. And beneath him was polished paintwork with the feel of metal.

Where am I?

How did I get here?

Then he realized with horror what must have happened.

He had diminished. At the wrong time, in the wrong place, he had diminished. But how? But why?

Then he remembered. . . .

He felt the rush of air that had preceded the crash, heard the colossal noise that had followed, metal ramming metal.

I should be dead.

A wave of pain came over him and once more he ceased to think.

The next time he regained consciousness, he tried to see more. Identifying what was close to him, other than his own self, was strangely difficult. So he focused on as long a range as he could manage. He was fuzzily aware of streetlamps and shop fronts signaling a town.

Then he saw the face of a clock high up in a stone clock tower. It seemed very far away but so large that its golden digits were clearly visible.

That was his point of reference.

When I raise my head I can see the face of an enormous clock.

And the clock is in a tower made of stone.

And the tower is in, is in . . . ?

The middle of the road.

He had seen that clock before, the clock of a country town, a place he had visited with Tonitheen on a summer's afternoon. *Morpeth*, he thought, *I am in Morpeth.*

He drew his gaze closer and closer to himself again, being sure to miss nothing in between. But as his gaze shifted to the nearer ground it became increasingly difficult to make out what he was seeing. It was like looking through a microscope and seeing specks of dirt the size of boulders. He failed, rested, and prepared to start again. Far distance, middle distance, and then . . . ?

Over and over and over again he moved his eyes from the recognizable clock to the mysterious place where he was lodged. He soon deduced that his own size was the problem, his own relationship to the things about him. This should never have happened. His size now was what was needed for inside the spaceship. It was totally out of kilter with the planet Earth.

His eyes still kept shifting from the clock to the thing he was holding on to, focusing out and in, and out and in, over and over again. And meanwhile his brain sifted all the information he could recall while his heart cried out for his lost son, and other emotions including raw fear and dazed bewilderment made him feel utterly fuddled.

He was still unable to get the focus right. The clock, the tower, the street, the chemist's shop with *Moss* written in large letters above its window, a lamppost, a stationary car somewhere down the road, another one further away.

But where am I? Where do I figure in this scene?

Eventually it was his reason that told him the answer.

His eyes were simply not equal to the task of recognition as he looked up at the windscreen wiper. It could have been the arm of a giant crane, the sort that stands on the dockside. Reason told him that this nearby, tangible object had to be much smaller than the clock. The polished metal beneath him seemed to slope downward into infinity.

Then, as a stroke of luck, the headlights of a passing truck flashed on a silver metal circle projecting from the lower side of the slope; unmistakably, it was the Mercedes insignia. The clue was not a very good one, but sufficient for Vateelin's desperate thoughts to turn it to good use.

This is a car.

I am sitting on the bonnet of a Mercedes, close to the windscreen, and this projection I am clinging to must be part of the base of the windscreen wiper.

Then there followed hours of thinking, deep into the night. He curled himself up in the corner of the wiper blade and began methodically to try to work things out.

What he must do was find the spaceship. That was the only way he could be sure of solving the problem of his discordant size. His chances of finding Tonitheen depended on it.

With a pang of guilt Vateelin remembered his failure to give his son proper instructions on what to do in just such a situation as this.

He knows that our names are keys.

He knows that in the direst of circumstances he must reveal them. They are his signal to me. He can guess that—without my having told him more.

He need not know how it works.

Tonitheen is clever and resourceful.

Vateelin went through a whole catalog of self-comfort. What he knew was that somehow his son must broadcast the names so that the spaceship would pick them up, detect where they came from, and retain them as a sort of homing device, to serve till time ran out.

And time would run out on the twenty-sixth of December. That was the day on which the spaceship was programmed to begin its return journey to Ormingat. In a perfectly neat and tidy situation, he and his son should have been safely established inside the vessel at least a week before liftoff. The twenty-sixth was the extreme limit. Vateelin himself did not know what would happen if they failed to reach the spaceship before then. The thought made him aware of his own culpable stupidity.

He looked down at his watch. It was two-thirty, already Saturday, the nineteenth of December—exactly a week to go. No problem for someone big enough to get on a train and travel north, no problem for someone big enough to walk to a station ten human minutes away. But for Vateelin merely to descend from the bonnet of a car apparently left parked for the night was a problem not yet solved and perhaps insoluble.

Chapter 17

Finding a Way

Vateelin had been trained never to panic in the face of the unexpected.

Even without training, that would have been part of his nature. Panic is a sort of despair and Vateelin was naturally hopeful. He knew that the worst *could* happen, and sometimes did. Keldu had died, leaving him desolate. Yet that was no reason to expect the worst, to give up without a fight. Keldu had fought to the end.

Vateelin's position against the hub of the wiper was reasonably secure and not too uncomfortable. He sat back and gave quiet thought to his situation.

The car was stationary and there was every hope that it would remain so at least till morning. It had been parked for long enough now to suggest that its driver could be staying in Morpeth overnight.

If his guess about the driver was correct, there should be at least a further three hours before he needed to move.

But it would be necessary to be clear of the car before it had the chance to go elsewhere. *I am here in a town I know. In it there is a mainline station. Trains go north from here to Edinburgh. Edinburgh is where I need to be.*

So . . .

He would have to get to the ground and find some way of reaching the station.

It was a strange situation to be in. He could look down at himself and see an ordinary human body clad in ordinary human clothes. He could feel the document case in his pocket. Everything about him was totally intact. He still felt bruised and sore but he could move his limbs. There were, he felt sure, no broken bones.

It was the problem of size that was staggering. Never before had he faced a situation in which he was so dysfunctional.

To cross the road would be a long journey. It would take time, and time is a limited resource.

It occurred to him that thinking he had till the twenty-sixth of the month was probably to give himself too great a leeway. *Where is Tonitheen? What is he doing? How is he coping with being alone?*

Vateelin knew that his son had not been hit by the tanker. He had seen him reach the pavement in that split second when everything had happened. What he did after that, his father could only guess, and one guess fought against another for probability.

Vateelin knew he had little hope of finding his son without the aid of the spaceship, especially not in his present situation. So what mattered now was to get to the ship with the least delay possible.

Vateelin clenched his fists and fought desperation.

One step at a time, he thought, *one step at a time.*

Don't think about getting to the station till you have got down from this car.

The car was a Mercedes—his glimpse of the emblem had told him so much. So he set himself to think of the form of the Mercedes and to consider whether it would be best to slide forward to the emblem and descend from there, or to find some way of abseiling down the side. He decided on the latter. The emblem was too far away. To slide in a straight line, and to control his speed on the shiny slope, was not something he was sure of being able to do.

For abseiling, he would need some sort of rope. Carefully, so as not to lose it, Vateelin took off his coat and wedged it beside the wiper. Then he removed the sweater he was wearing underneath. After putting his coat on again, he sat back and set to work. He bit the wool at the bottom of the sweater so that he had a loose thread and then he began to unravel the knitting and roll the wool into a ball. Once finished, he tied one end of the wool securely round a tiny projection on the windscreen wiper. The ball he held in both hands, ready to play out the yarn as he slid toward the side of the bonnet.

A good enough plan, perhaps, but the rope was not long enough!

It was just sufficient to take Vateelin over the edge. His distance from the ground was awesome; to fall would be for him the equivalent of jumping from a skyscraper.

Vateelin hung there like a spider hanging from a thread. He looked toward the ground, which was far away and too dark to make out clearly. He gripped the wool tightly and was filled with fear.

To let go and fall to the ground would take courage, but what alternative was there?

Then he thought, *There are two things in my favor. Being small can be an advantage—big things fall much harder. And I have been hurt so much now that a few extra bruises will make little difference.*

He took a deep breath, let go with both hands, and plunged downward, spinning round and round, before reaching the road and rolling toward the gutter. There he lay for over an hour, dazed and bruised.

 The next time he looked at his watch it was twenty past five.

The Mercedes had not moved. It rose up before him like the north face of the Eiger. One happy thought came to him as he crouched in the gutter: *At least I won't have to do that again.*

He tried to apply some logistics to the task before him. The railway station would have to be his objective. Up the street he was on, turn right at the junction, along another street, turn left up the hill, and there would be the station. But given that Vateelin's size bore no relation to the space to be traveled, it might as well have been a million miles away.

He looked at the world before him, a much more limited world than he had been able to see from the bonnet of the car. A cleft in the stone where he was sheltering he deduced to be at the point where two curbstones met. Taking a longer view, he was aware of the iron edge of a grating and gasped as he realized how near he had been to ending up somewhere in the sewers. And could still, could still, at one false step. So he had to stay close to the curb, close to the angle with the gutter.

Then what? Begin a valiant walk in what would seem to be the right direction? He set out to reach the back of the car, to give himself a clear view of the roadway. It took ages and his limbs hurt each step of the way.

Vateelin stopped to rest, looked at the small distance he had covered, and groaned. Walking to the South Pole would be about the normal human equivalent of reaching the station, or so it seemed to him now.

Chapter 18

Hitching a Lift

It was daylight and Vateelin's watch informed him that it was already eight-thirty. Things were moving. The world above was becoming populous. Sounds increased, distant, echoing and unidentifiable. What could he see? To his right, not far away, were the rear wheels of the blue Mercedes. In the road, cars were going in the direction he would have to follow, but at the junction some would go left, some right, and some straight ahead. Hitching a lift on a moving vehicle would be truly impossible, athletic beyond belief. Hitching a lift on a stationary vehicle was pointless, for who could know when or where it would go?

Gingerly Vateelin stepped away from the safety of the gutter and looked up at the pavement, where already people were walking, though not as many as in Casselton.

This was a small town on a Saturday morning. Vateelin noted a man with an umbrella over his arm, a boy carrying a sack full of newspapers, a woman pushing a pram. There would be more passersby, more and more of them as the shops opened. Hitch a lift on a person? Several persons. On and off and on, depending on the direction they took. People with shoelaces would be best. Take a leap for the lace and hang on tight.

Provided he could keep the directions clear in his head and observe the clues he knew how to look for, the plan seemed not such a bad one. It had another merit, of course. It was the only one!

At the noise of the Mercedes' engine starting, Vateelin leaped toward the curb again and began his climb up the space between the curbstones, bracing his back against one and using his feet against the other to propel him. In a short time he reached the pavement and crouched ready to jump as soon as a suitable shoe, traveling at a reasonable speed in the right direction, should present itself.

✵ The first suitable shoe was on the foot of a little girl walking with her mother. It was easy for Vateelin to leap onto the upper and cling to the swath of lace that had been tied into a large, floppy bow. The child was dawdling and being pulled away from the curb by her harassed parent.

They continued to the corner of the street, where a signpost informed travelers that the station was somewhere along a road to the right. The little girl and her mother turned left. Vateelin, nerves tensed, felt the turn, and knew from the map in his head that the change of direction was wrong for him. He jumped down onto the pavement, scuttled to the edge, and waited for another lift. Someone would have to be crossing the road.

Oh, wonder of wonders, someone was! It was a boy on a bicycle. He put one foot to the ground and was looking carefully before crossing. The bicycle's front wheel pointed in the direction of the station. Vateelin, just in time, sprang onto the boy's shoe and was carried up with the pedal as the cycle set off across the junction.

Unfortunately, success was short-lived. It was not long before they came to the side road that led toward the station. The boy pedaled straight past, remaining on the shopping street. Vateelin was stuck. He knew what was happening, but he was trapped. He was going up and down with the shoe on the pedal, an experience that can only be compared to whizzing round on a demented Ferris wheel. It was impossible to leap from there to the ground. Even at its lowest point the pedal was too high and it was moving much too fast.

The station road was left behind them. It was heartbreaking to be so near and yet so far away—and getting farther still. Then a set of traffic lights had the grace to turn red. The boy dropped his foot to the ground. Vateelin took a deep breath and hurled himself in the direction of the pavement.

This time he found himself at the foot of a lamppost. The pavement was busy with people. Vateelin shook himself and breathed deeply before he tried to work out how to retrace the distance to the turning for the station. Survival increases determination. *I know where I must go and faith will take me there.*

There would surely be another opportunity, another cycle slowing down, another shoe on a dawdling foot.

But what happened next was totally unexpected. All the light of the world was suddenly eclipsed.

Vateelin felt warm air breathing down at him through the darkness. He was, though he did not know it, looking up at the muzzle of a dog, a snuffling, bristly dog investigating the smells beneath the lamppost, tongue out and ready to lick the dirt.

Vateelin jumped back out of the shadow and gasped as he saw dog face, dog teeth, dog jaws! One thoughtless flick of that long red tongue, one gulp of the throat, and he would be in the creature's belly!

Terror shook Vateelin from head to foot. He was still in the body of a man, still his own size to himself. His smallness did not make him feel safe. The tongue was ready to lick him up. There was no time to turn and run. He threw himself to one side, leaping upward, just as he had done when the tanker crashed.

And this time he landed on his size ten feet, a solid, grown human being, suddenly, almost intrusively, visible to man and beast.

The dog gave a yelp of terror, turned tail, and ran back to its master. And only the dog had any inkling of what had really happened.

A woman with a basket walked straight into Patrick and glared at him.

"You want to watch where you're going," she snapped, but hurried on and said no more when she saw the state he was in. His coat was filthy, his face was all bruised, and his fair hair was matted with dirt. Canty would not have recognized his "well-off" friend!

Others on the street were aware of seeing someone they had not noticed before, someone of disreputable appearance who would be best avoided. If they were startled, they could not relate this to seeing the stranger materialize from nothing. That sort of thing simply does not happen.

But it does and it did! Patrick smiled a smile that reached from his lips right down to his toes. *I have survived. I have survived. Whatever happens now, I can win.*

Chapter 19

Catching a Train

Patrick turned to walk in the direction of the road that led off to the railway station. He walked, as he had always walked in this manifestation, with his head held high and his stride purposeful. The triumph of his return to his normal Earth size, together with his anxiety to reach his destination, gave him speed and helped him to become temporarily unaware of all the bruising his body had suffered and all the pain he would still have to endure.

People stepped aside as he passed. They looked at him furtively. His strength was evident in his every movement; the bloody face and stubbly chin, the matted hair and filthy clothes gave him a threatening appearance. He was a man who had evidently been in some sort of fight and he looked intimidating.

Of all this, Patrick was totally unaware. He knew only that he must go to the station and catch the first train to Edinburgh. On the less crowded pavement that led to the station he almost broke into a run. Then, for the first time, he realized that he was not perfectly fit. His legs suddenly felt weak at the knees and his back was painful. He winced but kept on walking as fast as he was able.

He was very relieved to see the entrance to the station. To sit on a train for an hour or so would be such a comfort.

He looked at the timetable and discovered that the next train stopping there on its way north would depart at twelve-thirty. His watch, shockproof and undamaged, told him that it was now ten past twelve.

Once on the platform, he took his wallet from his pocket and checked that his ticket to Edinburgh had survived the ordeal they had both been through. It had. His money was also intact. All in all, things could have been worse.

Patrick was so wrapped up in thought and so concerned about the really important things that he failed to notice his own condition and was quite oblivious to the glances others cast in his direction. When the train came he found an unreserved seat in the first-class compartment and settled down to rest. The carriage was nearly empty. No one came and sat beside him. *Peace*, he thought, *perfect peace.*

Then he looked up to see the ticket collector pausing to check his ticket. He was a youngish man, with eyes that were probably naturally protruding, but seeing Patrick made them appear even more startled.

Patrick passed the ticket to him and smiled. The smile hurt a little and he remembered wiping his mouth with his handkerchief.

The ticket collector inspected the ticket and then looked dubiously at the passenger.

"This ticket is from Casselton, sir," he said warily. He did not want to provoke an incident. If it was necessary to call for help, he would do so quietly. The passenger's appearance was not that normally seen in any part of the train, and certainly not in a first-class compartment. *Proceed with caution.*

"Is that a problem?" said Patrick. "I am, after all, making a shorter journey. I just happened to be in Morpeth last night and it was easier to travel from here than to go back home."

Patrick's tone and manner did not assort well with his bedraggled clothes and battered face. He sounded self-assured but at the same time quite kindly.

The ticket collector, who was fairly new to the job, had a moment of uncertainty.

"You seem to have met with an accident," he ventured to say. Then, for the first time, Patrick looked down at his hands, all scraped and grubby, and his cuffs, caked with mud. It took him seconds to recover his poise.

"Yes," he said lightly. "I fell on the way to the station. Lucky not to break anything."

"A bad fall," said the ticket collector. "Do you need help?"

"No," said Patrick. "I'll be perfectly all right—see to everything when I get to Edinburgh."

There was nothing more for the collector to say. He still felt dubious and was pleased that the carriage was not crowded.

After he had gone, Patrick made his way to the lavatory. He might be in a bad state. Certainly the aches and pains were making themselves felt. But soap and water would surely help.

As he fastened the door behind him, he caught sight of himself full-length in the mirror and gasped. *Ye gods,* he thought, *it's a wonder I've managed to get this far! I look bad enough to be arrested!*

He rested both hands on the washbasin, looked sideways into the mirror again, and then burst into laughter. He thought of the little ticket collector with his brown eyes bulging and saying so politely, *You seem to have met with an accident. . . .*

Tears of laughter rolled down Patrick's face and the saltiness of them stung his swollen lip. That brought him up short and sobered him.

He looked straight at himself and considered what improvements he could make with the limited resources available.

The matted hair first. He took a paper towel and soaked it, then squeezed water into his hair till it was wet enough to be soaped. Liquid soap. More water. More paper towels. After a great deal of effort, his hair was almost back to its normal fairness. He took his comb from his pocket and combed it into place. It was still wet, of course, but at least it wasn't scruffy anymore.

Next, very gingerly, he washed his face. The bruising

and the scrapes were extensive. His swollen lip snarled at him. He very soon gave up any attempt to make things better as he became aware that too much rubbing might make them worse. His chin began to bleed and he had to dab it dry.

Someone tried the lavatory door and a child's voice called out, "There's still somebody in, Mummy. Unless the door's jammed."

"Try another one, Brenda," said the parent impatiently, "and do stop making a fuss."

Patrick coughed loudly to indicate his presence.

His coat was another problem. To remove it would be very difficult because his arms were stiff and aching. In any case, he would not want to carry it in this cold weather. He was already regretting the loss of his sweater. The caked mud he tried brushing off with dry towels, but he did not have much success. And he had enough sense to know that wetting the mud could be disastrous. So he made his way back to his seat and settled behind the free copy of *The Guardian* that the company had provided.

Without coming from behind the broadsheet, he accepted the complimentary coffee and drank it gratefully.

The journey soon over. His slow and painful ablutions had helped the time to pass.

"Passengers for Edinburgh Waverley," said the voice on the P.A. system. Patrick stood up, fastened his coat, and climbed down onto the platform. Each thing done is one thing less to do.

Chapter 20

A Visitor

It was just after ten o'clock on Saturday morning when Jamie left the ward, taking his genius with him. The game, short-lived, was over. Thomas was a very sad and lonely little boy once more. To use his alien voice to startle and impress people was no longer funny. He felt more forsaken than ever.

He lay still in his bed in the quiet ward, thinking.

He was not scheming or planning, just suddenly and profoundly aware of two things: *I am, and always will be, a stranger on this planet; no love I have for any other being is greater than my love for Vateelin.*

He is my father, the only one of my true family that I know. "Oh, Vateelin, Vateelin *mesht*," he murmured, but so softly that only the pillow could have heard.

To speak in the voice of Ormingat to these people in the hospital now seemed shabby and paltry, making a game of such a deep reality.

So what next?

Return to silence. The keys *might* work through telepathy. They could as easily work through telepathy as through sound. Either way was impossible to understand. It was all guesswork.

Thomas decided to think and think and think the words, to say them silently inside his head. *Vateelin Tonitheen Ormingat—Ormingat Tonitheen Vateelin—Vateelin Tonitheen Ormingat—Ormingat Tonitheen Vateelin—Vateelin Tonitheen Ormingat—Ormingat Tonitheen Vateelin.*

Then wait. Then try again.

In the ward there was a Mickey Mouse clock on the wall. Its pointers were Mickey's large gloved hands. The mouse's forefingers pointed to the numbers, the hour arm shorter than the minute one. Thomas began watching and waiting for the long arm to reach the hour, the quarter, the half hour. And at each quarter he recited inwardly his mantra: *Vateelin Tonitheen Ormingat—Ormingat Tonitheen Vateelin—Vateelin Tonitheen Ormingat—Ormingat Tonitheen Vateelin—Vateelin Tonitheen Ormingat—Ormingat Tonitheen Vateelin.*

Kirsty was busy with the younger children at the other end of the ward and it was some time before she could come and give any attention to Thomas. Besides, the staff had all been told to give him "space." So when she finally came to his bedside, it was ten minutes past twelve, nearly time for lunch.

"Would you like to get dressed?" she said brightly. "There's no reason why you shouldn't. And you can eat at the center table if you like. Evie will be having her lunch there—she's the one in the far corner with the bandages round her head. And Joseph wants to come to the table, even though his leg is in plaster.''

Thomas did not answer.

Kirsty got his own clothes out of the locker and handed them to him.

"I'll draw your curtain and leave you to get ready in peace. The trolley will be round with the lunches in about twenty minutes. It's not a bad meal and you do have some choice. Just tick what you'd like on this list.''

She put a pencil in his hand and guided him through the choices. He ticked obediently but neither smiled nor spoke. He should perhaps have pretended to be unable to read, but total, consistent abstraction is very difficult when you are only eleven years old.

After Kirsty left him he put on his clothes, folded the hospital pajamas neatly, and laid them across the foot of the bed. Then he sat in the chair and waited. He did not even bother to open the curtain.

When Kirsty came and ushered him to the table he sat down. The other two children were already there. The meal was eaten in near-silence. The boy with his leg in plaster stared down at his plate and said aggressively, "I'm going home tomorrow, so there!" No one answered him.

Evie mentioned that she had a rabbit called Fred, but since neither of her companions showed any interest in this information, she began to make hills with her mashed potato and let gravy rivers flow between them.

Thomas never spoke at all.

After lunch he returned to his chair. Kirsty asked him nicely if he would like to do a jigsaw puzzle or play with the Lego bricks in the tray on the table. When he did not answer, she brought a Batman annual and a pile of comics and placed them on his bedside table.

So Thomas was given more "space." He watched the Mickey Mouse clock and went listlessly back to his effort at telepathy, though with no real hope that it would work. *Vateelin Tonitheen Ormingat—Ormingat Tonitheen Vateelin—Vateelin Tonitheen Ormingat—Ormingat Tonitheen Vateelin—Vateelin Tonitheen Ormingat—Ormingat Tonitheen Vateelin.*

And between the quarter hours, he flicked over pages in the annual, felt deeply sad, and was startled once when a tear fell on the page, making a splotch on the Batmobile. He turned several pages rapidly to hide it.

At three o'clock something happened. A tall man about Patrick's age, slim-built with dark hair and a mustache, walked briskly into the ward and was directed to Thomas's bed. Ernie made to accompany him, but the man said, "It's all right, I'll do my own introduction."

"You know about the—er—voice?" said Ernie, hoping that the visitor had some understanding of children.

"I've been briefed," he said. "Dr. Ramsay showed me the notes and I've had a word with Nurse West."

The visitor came to where Thomas was sitting. He pulled up another chair from beside the bed that had been Jamie's and sat down beside the boy, who looked at him guardedly.

"I'm Inspector Galway," said the man as he clasped his hands in front of him. "I could tell you a lot more about me and try to be really matey, but it's a waste of time. Either you want to help me or you don't. That's the way I see it."

Thomas looked at him, meeting his eyes but still saying nothing.

"Well, at least you're listening," said the inspector. "So let me explain just why I am here."

He looked round and then half pulled the curtain, as if to give them a little privacy, or at least to indicate to the nurses that this was to be a private conversation.

"I have some questions that are hard to answer," said Inspector Galway, "and it just might be that you can help. For a start, it would be nice to know your real name. I don't think it's Sammy."

Thomas said nothing but could not help shaking his head. It would be nice to get rid of that name.

"Well," said the inspector, "that's one thing cleared up. You are not called Sammy and neither is your surname Bentley."

Thomas nodded agreement. He had made up his mind not to speak at all. To speak seemed to him too fraught with problems. He felt that he had said too much already.

"So what is your name?" said the inspector. "You do

hear me but I am not about to play silly games with you. This isn't Rumpelstilstkin, if you know what I mean."

The man was being so reasonable and sensible that Thomas felt like talking to him but by this time he had twisted his thoughts into such a knot that he was afraid to say anything.

"If we know your name," said the inspector, ignoring the silence, "we can find out where you belong. We can trace your people."

The inspector had interviewed boys before, boys from the poorest parts of town. He had the habit of not specifying "mam" or "dad" or even "parents." They were things he knew not every child possessed and so he was careful.

But Thomas heard the words "we can trace your people" and was instantly alarmed. Was he about to betray the secret of Ormingat? Had he—dreadful thought—betrayed it already?

He looked down at his hands and decided not even to nod or shake his head, not even to look as if he were listening. The inspector waited less and less patiently. Then he got up and replaced the chair he had been sitting on.

"I can't help you, son, if you won't help me," he said. The inspector turned his back on Thomas and went to the desk.

Ernie was carefully filling in a chart. He stopped on the inspector's approach.

"Any luck?" he said.

"None whatsoever," said Inspector Galway. "His

name's not Sammy Bentley, but I only got that from a nod of the head. And we really knew that already."

"So you didn't hear the voice," said Ernie. "I thought you mustn't have. It travels quite a long way."

"No voice, not a sound," said the inspector. "I'm off duty tomorrow, but I'll give it another try on Monday if nothing happens in between. I'm going upstairs to see the brewery men next. They are adamant about having run a man over even though there is no sign of a body."

Inspector Galway smiled slightly.

"Still, it is a nice sort of mystery," he said. "A murder with a missing body, I have actually met before. A road accident with a missing body must be a first. I might bring the piece of sheepskin in and show it to your patient on Monday. Shock tactics."

Ernie was angry. He knew nothing about the sheepskin, but he could not approve of anyone who would so glibly offer to use shock tactics on a child.

"I think you will be advised not to do that," he said quietly. "I cannot see Dr. Ramsay permitting it. The boy, after all, is Dr. Ramsay's patient."

Inspector Galway looked abashed.

"You're probably right," he said. "It was just a passing thought, not one of my better ones! But it *would* be nice to know some of the answers."

Thomas spent the rest of the evening worrying. Getting ready for bed was done in total silence. Cornelia was back on duty. She said good night to him, even offered to read him a story, but took his silence as a refusal.

"No nightmares," she said as she left him. "Not for you . . . and not for anybody else either!"

She smiled at him, but he very deliberately turned his head away.

Chapter 21

Gibson's Pharmacy

Patrick walked up the ramped pavement and out of the station. Alongside him walked dozens of other people who did not even observe his dirty, ragged coat and his injured face. This was Edinburgh on the busiest Saturday of the year and, with the sophistication of a capital city, it welcomed all and noticed none. Patrick pulled his collar up against the cold and was grateful.

His limbs hurt and his walk was stiff and wearisome. Added to this, his head began to throb. His one thought was to find a chemist's shop somewhere and purchase some painkillers. There was no way he could think straight without getting rid of at least some of the pain.

There was, naturally, no question of going straight to the spaceship. It was in the earth beneath the Scott Monument. It had been there for five years. Its density would have made it sink well down into the topsoil. Patrick would have to dig to reach it. For now—minor point, perhaps—his hands felt too sore for digging, though he was glad to feel the trowel still safely lodged in his pocket. For now—major point—Princes Street and all the area around the monument would be full of people coming and going. It would definitely be dangerous to be seen digging a hole in that particular place!

It was a quarter to three and already dusk when Patrick came out of the station. He had some recollection of little shops in the area behind the station, little shops that might well include a chemist's. So that was the way he went. Without even looking toward Princes Street, he walked over the bridge in the opposite direction.

It took quite some time to find a pharmacy, but when he did, it was exactly what he was looking for. In his state he would have felt wary of going into a glossy Boots in the middle of Princes Street.

Gibson's Pharmacy, small and old-fashioned, was much better. He went in.

The bell above the door jangled. A gray-haired woman behind the counter looked up from a box she was tidying, saw the customer, and was slightly alarmed.

"Yes?" she said.

"Aspirins," said Patrick, coming to the counter. "I have had an accident and, to be frank, I'm aching all over."

"An accident, now," said the woman slowly. "It's a wonder you haven't gone to the infirmary, the state you're in. Would you like to sit down? I'll get Mr. Gibson to have a word with you."

She indicated a dark wood chair to the right of the counter. Patrick by now felt dizzy with pain and was glad to do as she suggested, no matter what questions might follow.

"Mr. Gibson," the assistant called, "can you be having a word with this young man? He's in a sorry state."

From the back of the shop came an old man with wispy gray hair and pale blue eyes.

"All right, Edna," he said. "I'll see to him."

He came from behind the counter and looked closely at Patrick.

"You *have* been in the wars," he said. "How did all this happen?"

"I had a bad fall," said Patrick. "Just before I got on the train. I couldn't stop to see to anything or I'd have missed it."

"Well," said the chemist dubiously, "a bad fall? You can call it that—none of my business, really. But I think you should be seeing a doctor. Falls can cause concussion, you know, and you might need a jab for the tetanus."

"I'll see a doctor later," said Patrick. "But for now, I'd be grateful if you could let me have something for the pain."

Patrick's face was full of misery. Involuntarily he squeezed his eyes shut and bit his lip. The chemist shook his head like the wise old man he was and felt sorry for this lad who was young enough to be his son.

"A cup of tea," he said, "a rest in the back room, and a bit of a wash and brush-up. Oh, and the painkillers. We'll not forget them. Go and put the kettle on, Edna."

The elderly assistant sniffed and went to do as she was bid. George Gibson was a soft touch, and no mistake! It would surely have been enough to give the young fellow advice, sell him something, and send him on his way. She was as charitable as the next person, but she was much more aware than her employer of the dictum that says you have to draw the line somewhere!

The tea was made and poured. The shop bell jangled again and Edna went to serve another customer.

"So how did it really happen?" said George as he cleaned up the wounds on Patrick's face, neck, and hands. "Been in a fight?"

Patrick looked him straight in the eye and said, "I know that's what it must look like, but I haven't. I appreciate what you're doing for me and I'm only sorry I can't tell you the truth. But the truth would be much too hard for you to believe."

"Try me," said the chemist with a smile.

"Would you mind very much if I didn't?" said Patrick. "All I can really say is that I have had a genuine accident. I'm not a criminal and I haven't been in a fight."

"All right," said George. "Now, if you can just take your coat off, I'll get Edna to give it a bit of a brush for you."

Edna had just returned from the front shop, determined to keep an eye on things. When she heard George's words, she was not what one might call pleased. She took the coat from her employer and went into the front shop, where she yanked a stiff clothes brush from the stand where it was one of three up for sale. Returning to the back room, she spread a copy of *The Scotsman* over the floor. Then she thumped away at the caked mud with a vigor that owed much to indignation. The newspaper was soon covered with grains of brown earth.

Patrick sat in his shirtsleeves by the electric fire, shivering slightly and feeling increasingly embarrassed. He had taken two painkillers and drunk a mug of strong, sweet tea. His head was easing and he was becoming less helpless.

"I'm sorry to put you both to all this trouble," he said. "You are truly good Samaritans. I can't say how much I appreciate your help."

"I'm sure you do," said Edna sharply. "It'd be surprising if you didn't."

But there was worse to come.

"Do you need a room for the night? My sister can put you up. I can give her a ring if you like," said the chemist as Patrick took his coat from Edna and began carefully to pull it on, wincing at the pain in his hands.

Edna glared at both of them.

Patrick said quickly, "No, no. I'm very grateful for the offer, but I am expected elsewhere. I think you've set me up well enough now to be on my way."

"Well," said the chemist, smiling, "I suppose if you're expected at that place called 'elsewhere,' elsewhere is where you must be going!"

"What do I owe you?" said Patrick, getting out his wallet.

"Let me see," said the chemist, wary of Edna's accusing gaze, "there's two pounds twenty for the painkillers and a pound sixty-five for the balm—make it myself, you know. As good as any of the proprietary brands and a sight cheaper. That'll be three eighty-five altogether. You can pay Edna in the front shop."

"But . . ." began Patrick, wondering what to say next. In his time on Earth, he had found repeatedly how wonderfully kind ordinary people could be.

"Nothing for the tea and sympathy," said George. "We Samaritans don't charge for them!"

Patrick smiled at the older man and said a heartfelt thanks.

When the door clanged behind their strange customer, George looked at Edna and said sternly, "Judge not, that ye be not judged."

Chapter 22

The Scott Monument

Patrick looked a little more respectable when he left
Gibson's shop. The coat was still badly stained, but at
least it was free of caked mud. The hemline was jagged
but comparatively unremarkable. His face was still
bruised and sore, his knuckles still scraped. He walked
stiffly, still in some pain, but he felt that the worst was
over.

As he crossed the railway bridge, he had his first
direct view of Princes Street.

Then he saw it!

Where Sir Walter Scott's great monument should
have been, there was something with an outline like a
small-scale skyscraper. From top to bottom it was
squared off with boards and scaffolding.

Patrick gasped, terrifyingly aware of the possible im-
plications. Five years ago it had looked so different.
The way back to the spaceship, not especially easy, had
nevertheless seemed quite clear. Now what?

He walked quickly on, across the road outside the station, into the nearest gate and past the Livingstone statue. The spaceship, he knew, was in a spot almost exactly halfway between a large old beech tree and the spiked railings and gate that edged the park on Princes Street. The tree was there, unchanged, outside the structure guarding the monument. A quick check filled Patrick with relief. The patch of earth where the spaceship was buried was also left outside the barrier! On a panel above the very spot, a portrait of the statue's designer, George Meikle Kemp, looked down.

Patrick sat on a park bench near the scaffolding and paused to consider what to do next.

This was the Saturday before Christmas. Edinburgh was full of people and buses and cars. The shops were festive and Princes Street glittered. *Yes, Patrick, this is where you inadvertently landed the spaceship. And there it still is, beside the shrouded monument, sunk two or maybe three feet under the ground. Small it might be, but that orb is very dense.*

As he sat there, Patrick became increasingly aware of how tired he was. What he needed now was what George Gibson had offered—a bed for the night.

If he had been able to enter the spaceship, all of the power of Ormingat would have been there at his fingertips. He could have summoned energy and healing, created any illusion his present problems might call for, and, most important of all, searched the scanner for a message from his son. Instead, he was stuck just yards away from it and unable to do anything but sit and yawn.

He had money, though, a wallet full of notes.

After he had sat for half an hour, struggling not to fall asleep, the answer became obvious. He must book into a hotel, have a nice warm bath, and go to bed.

Booking into a hotel in his present state might not be easy. No real luggage—he could hardly count his document case as such—a dirty sheepskin coat, and a face that looked as if it had been in a fight. There would be no room at the inn for anyone looking like that!

Then he thought of his credit card, still tucked in the wallet. He had not intended to use it again, but these were special circumstances. In all his time on Earth, he had never paid a credit card bill, had never received one. The account was dealt with elsewhere in the system. Patrick had known his limit, a generous one, and had never overspent.

Despite his tiredness, he summoned up enough energy to walk along the main street and into the side streets and squares, looking for a suitable place to stay. It was not long before he found the ideal hotel, a very respectable-looking building on a square overlooking pleasant gardens. *Maitland Manor* was written in small-ish electric lettering across the front door. And, more important than the name, underneath was a telephone number.

Patrick went to the telephone box in the next street and rang the number.

"Maitland's," said a terse male voice on the other end of the line. "Can I help you?"

"I'd like a room for the night," said Patrick, "a single room for tonight." Then as an afterthought he added, "And tomorrow night. I'll pay in advance by credit card, if that would suit."

Patrick's voice on the telephone sounded right, no hint in it of anything untoward. And two nights, as Patrick suspected, were less open to suspicion than one might have been. To pay in advance by credit card was certainly acceptable.

"We have, as it happens, just the one room," said the voice. "You're lucky there. It's a busy time of year, you know."

"Yes," said Patrick, "I realize that. I had to come to Edinburgh at very short notice. There is still business I must attend to. I may be quite late arriving. That will, I hope, be no problem?"

"None at all," said the voice.

When everything was settled, Patrick set out to take care of what he felt he needed before he could present himself at the hotel. Sometime after eleven seemed a good time—quiet, with night staff on duty and, he hoped, lights turned low. His aching limbs would have preferred an earlier hour, but prudence made the later time more sensible.

He walked back into Princes Street, going once more in the direction of Waverley Station. He got as far as the little bookshop just opposite the monument before stopping. Outside was an array of Scottish post-cards on a revolving stand. Inside were maps and guidebooks.

Patrick chose two postcards and took them to the counter.

"I don't remember the Scott monument being in that state the last time I was here," he said.

"Been like that since last year," said the assistant. "At first they just cordoned it off because it seemed to be crumbling. Then, so they say, the face fell off and nearly hit somebody. Whatever it was, they've found it's in much worse condition than they thought. Everyone's mystified, but they're determined to put it to rights."

Patrick shivered. He wondered if his spaceship had led to this rapid deterioration. No one from Ormingat would intentionally harm anything on Earth, but the universe is full of imponderables. The doubt, the mystery, would be something to report back. And if there was the least possibility that the cause was any vibration or emanation from the alien ship, then Ormingat would surely find a quiet way to compensate.

Next he went into the department store to buy a weekend bag. To fill it he bought some pajamas, a bathrobe for bulk, a shirt, and a change of underwear.

As he left the shop, Patrick was suddenly aware that his Earth body needed sustenance. He walked along till he came to a cozy-looking restaurant near the corner of a side street. He went to the counter, bought a bowl of stew and a pot of tea, then took his tray to a table near the fireplace, where he felt hidden by the projecting wooden mantelpiece. The food was good, but thoughts troubled every bite.

What is Thomas doing now? Where is he? Alone some-where? Frightened?

A waiter in a black beret and striped waistcoat came by and cleared the table next to him. Patrick kept his head down and concentrated upon pouring his tea.

Not harmed by the crash, so much I do know, but shocked, surely shocked. And lost. What would he do? Where would he go?

Patrick sat slowly drinking his tea and trying to guess what had happened to Thomas.

Would he be with Stella?

With Stella in Belthorp?

The wallpaper around the fireplace had a pattern of Japanese ladies looking graceful. Patrick looked up at them as he wiped the bread around the empty bowl and savored the last taste of the stew.

What a muddle, he thought with a sigh, *what a terrible, terrible muddle. . . .*

Finally he felt he could spin out his meal no further. He went into the street and wandered around, wondering what to do. It was still too early to risk going to the hotel.

Then he saw a cinema advertising a film about invaders from outer space. He went in, took a seat in the dark auditorium, and settled back to rest. On the screen, an alien with one huge eye in the middle of its scaly head was trying and failing to instill terror into a group of handsome, muscular scientists. Patrick nodded, then slept.

* * *

142

Checking into the Maitland was much easier than he could have hoped for. The man on the desk was reading a motoring magazine.

Patrick said, "My name's Derwent, Patrick Derwent. I made a reservation this afternoon."

"Just fill the form in," said the man, handing Patrick a card and a pen without ever looking up into his face. "I'll need to check your credit card."

Patrick wrote quickly, using the details he always used when the transaction involved the credit card. The man went on reading. The finished form was handed back. The man ran the credit card through his machine, then returned it to Patrick.

"Room seventeen," he said reaching blindly for the key from the wall behind him. "First floor. Lift's just to your left there, or there's the stairs if you'd rather. Morning call?"

"No, thank you," said Patrick, and he hurried away while the man got on with reading the article about the merits of the latest Volvo.

As he went into his room Patrick observed a card on the door handle, a means of ordering a breakfast tray. Patrick filled it in neatly, requesting that the tray be left at seven A.M. Then he hung it over the handle again and went in to retire for the night. Things were definitely getting better! After a good night's rest he would be able to tackle the problem of reaching the spaceship with a much clearer mind. He did not expect to sleep—there was too much to worry about—but at least he would be resting.

The hot bath was heavenly. The body Patrick inhabited expressed gratitude from its head to its aching feet. Afterward he made himself a pot of tea and lay on the bed in his new pajamas. His expectation of lying awake proved false. He yawned into the pillow and it was not long before he slept a deep and dreamless sleep. There is only so much worrying the mind can do.

In Casselton General Hospital, Thomas too was sleeping the sleep of exhaustion. He had called on his father and his father had not come. He had woven Ormingat names into a spell and the spell had failed.

Chapter 23

Sunday in Edinburgh

It was after eight o'clock when Patrick woke up. Hastily he rescued his tray from the corridor and went back into his room to eat breakfast. Outside, church bells were summoning people to morning services, though the day was barely dawning.

Patrick, feeling much stronger this morning, puzzled over what to do next. Approaching the spaceship's resting place in daylight he had already decided would be too risky. He thought fleetingly of taking a train back to Casselton, but what would be the good of that? To find Thomas would be just as impossible as it had been the night before, and, in the circumstances, downright dangerous.

The only logical way of being sure of finding his son was to return to the spaceship. All his eggs were in that one basket; all his faith was in the power of that ship's intellect—limited, mechanical, often irritatingly simple, but ultimately stronger than anything on Earth.

He did think of ringing Stella, but that too was impossible. It would have risked such a betrayal as had never happened in 250 years of Ormingat explorations. And Vateelin did not know how he would be able to manage the outcome.

Patrick Vateelin, two sides merging, sat on his bed with his head in his hands. Life was surely too difficult; its problems were insoluble. Too many things could go wrong. He thought of Thomas, alone in Casselton. Thomas, not Tonitheen. Eleven-year-old Earth child, lost and bewildered. There could surely be no greater failure than this. Patrick wept.

It was then that the spirit of Keldu hovered over him. He felt as if her hand were resting lovingly on his shoulder. Then a voice seemed to whisper, *"Ethalda, Vateelin kern. Inn-essoond midayla."*

"Argule," murmured Vateelin. His hand reached up to hers. There was nothing there. But she had left hope behind her, and Vateelin's heart seized on the hope and began planning for what should, what must be done.

He was glad he had booked the room for two nights. His attempt to reach the spaceship would have to be made in the early hours of the morning, after even the latest of revelers had gone home to bed.

Once within the ship, it would be easy.

Well, it would, wouldn't it?

Find the voice on the scan, Tonitheen's voice, home in on it, locate it to the nth. Then the ship must search

146

and find and rescue. It must be capable of that, or why had he always been taught that the words were keys? Why scan and find, if find did not mean rescue?

Patrick left the hotel just after nine-thirty. Apart from the sheepskin coat, which still looked somewhat raffish, his appearance was improving. The chemist's salve had taken the anger out of his scrapes and bruises. The hotel's shampoo had returned his hair to normal.

He walked out of the square onto Princes Street. There, about two hundred yards away, was Scott's hidden monument. And buried beneath the monument, in a mound of soil, lay an alien artifact, a beautiful, potent piece of buried treasure.

The day had turned bright, but the air was icy cold. Patrick turned up his collar of his coat and wished again that he had not parted with his woolen sweater.

He walked along Princes Street, beside the gardens, where people were already walking despite the coldness of the weather. When he came to the Scott Monument, he walked more slowly and scrutinized the boards around the base, all decorated with graffiti-defying pictures from Scottish history. A few yards further on and just round the corner was the exact spot where he would have to dig. It was no more than a foot from the wooden panels. Just one more foot and his task would have been impossible!

Patrick hoped the ship would not have sunk deep;

the longer the work took, the more danger there would be of detection.

As he gazed, he began remembering where the story began, six long years before. . . .

⭐ *We sat together in the darkness, awaiting the fresh energy that would come when the orbit of Ormingat was left behind. Tonitheen held my hand tightly, fearful and not really understanding. He was afraid of the dark, especially the enclosed dark in this new, unknown space.*

"We'll get used to it," I said. "In a while we'll have more light. There are pictures to watch of Earth, words to learn, all sorts of things to do. But for now, all the spaceship's energy is concentrated on gathering speed."

Tonitheen shivered, though the ship was warm enough. I put my arm around him and held him tight. Already the texture of his clothes had changed and the feel of his body was subtly different. As was mine. We were both undergoing the most awesome metamorphosis. Each thing that would leave the ship with us was becoming an Earth thing, obeying the same formula that was turning us into Earth beings. Hard for me to grasp, impossible for my child.

"We'll play," I said. "That'll pass the time. We'll play at being Earth people. You will be Thomas Derwent and I shall be your father, Patrick Derwent. We live in a village called Belthorp, in the north of England. When the power lights the screen, I'll show you where it is and what it looks like."

* * *

It was his father's turn to feel lost and lonely. For that moment hope drained away from Vateelin and he wondered if it would ever come right. There was still the business of being Patrick and somehow getting through another day. *Argule,* he prayed, *Argule essoond midayl.*

He walked into the gateway and sat down with the statue of Livingstone behind him and the portrait panel of Kemp in front. They had a presence there, and Patrick, Patrick Vateelin felt more than ever an intrusive alien. And perhaps a guilty alien, visiting destruction on this beautiful city.

"Bit parrrky, isn't it?" said a voice beside him. Patrick started and looked round to see that he had company. An elderly man, dressed in a thick tweed jacket and wearing a tartan cap, had sat down beside him.

"Still," he went on, "no worrrse than you can expect this time o' yearrr."

Patrick smiled at him bleakly.

"Go home and tell her you're sorry," said the man. "It's the best way. Shame to miss your Sunday dinner just for a bit of a tiff."

Patrick smiled again.

"Maybe you're right," he said, and got up to go.

"I *am* rrright," said the man. "Make no mistake about it!"

With such an admonition, Patrick decided that it would be inadvisable to stay within range of the helpful stranger. He got up, saluted briskly, and walked across the road to the shops. *Safety,* he thought, *in numbers. Better to be part of a crowd.*

So till the day was over, he walked around the shops, climbed the hill to the castle, ate lunch and high tea in different restaurants, and finally settled for the evening in a public bar to watch television.

And all the time he was thinking furiously.

The spaceship could be retrieved only at dead of night. The time between now and then was precious time inevitably wasted. Once inside the vessel Patrick would have six days—only six days to save his son and prepare to leave Earth. It was not, he told himself, impossible; but there he could not hope for an extension. At midnight on Saturday, he had been told at the start, the ship would detonate and scream off into space, with or without its passengers.

When Patrick returned to the hotel, he went to the desk and told the clerk he would be leaving at three in the morning.

"Will you be needing a taxi, sir?" said the clerk, a much more helpful young man than the night porter had been.

Patrick was about to say no when it occurred to him that yes would be a more sensible answer.

"Thank you," he said. "A taxi for three A.M. would be fine."

Chapter 24

"Little Boy Lost"

It was Sunday evening before any mention was made in the Martin household of the boy with the very strange voice.

Jamie's homecoming on the previous day had been as riotous and as noisy as everything else in Jamie's life.

There were two quiet beings in the household: Mrs. Martin, who would have liked them all to be quiet but couldn't manage it; and the dog, Calypso, than which, her owner maintained, a more cunning beast never walked the earth!

The drive home had been noisy enough: Six-year-old Carla and three-year-old Rodney sat jabbering in the back of the car with their mother. Jamie had the front seat next to his father. Determined to vie with the noises from behind him, Jamie reached into his bag and pulled out his musical keyboard. Once more the saints went marching in, putting up a good fight but not quite winning the battle of the decibels.

Once home, things got worse, not better.

Calypso had managed to invade the fridge and steal a pound of steak and a string of sausages.

"Get out of here, you horrible cur," yelled Mr. Martin when he saw the evidence strewn on the floor. "I'll skin you alive, I will."

The little white mongrel cringed and showed the whites of her eyes in melodramatic terror.

"Don't, Dad, please don't," said Carla at the top of her voice.

"I should have put the hook on the fridge door," said Mrs. Martin with a sigh. "It's not the dog's fault. She's only doing what's natural to her."

"And I am doing what comes naturally to me," said her husband. "That hound has nicked my dinner and I want revenge!"

He put on a look of extreme wickedness and now Rodney began to howl.

It was all an act, of course. Calypso was Dad's own dog, his best friend. No way would he really have hurt her.

Jamie stood beside the table, looking at them all, not feeling quite at home yet in a room with carpets: over the last three weeks antiseptic hospital floors had become the norm. Then the noise his family was making spurred him to action.

He banged on the table and said loudly, "I've *just* had the worst 'pendix in the country, prob'ly in the world. I've *just* come home. And you're all ignoring me. I think I'll go back to the hospital!"

The rest of them stopped in their tracks.

Mrs. Martin bent down to her son and put her arm round him. His shoulders felt narrower somehow and his fair-skinned face was very pale. Mrs. Martin felt tears coming to her eyes as she thought of the operation that had gone so frighteningly wrong.

"You're right, my love," she said. "Absolutely right. This should be your day. We are all so glad to have you home safe and well."

She frowned at her husband and added, "And nobody cares about a few crummy sausages and a chunk of mad cow! There's a special coming-home cake in the pantry. The cupboard's not what you'd call bare. I am going to make us all a party!"

So it was no wonder that no mention was made on that first day of the boy in the next bed with *that voice.*

On Sunday evening Mrs. Martin at last had time to recall her encounter with the boy in the next bed to Jamie. The younger children were both in bed. Jamie was allowed to stay up later, to sit with his parents and watch television. It was a quiet, civilized time, not without conversation; the television was often just something chuntering on in the background.

"I've never heard anything like that boy's voice,"

said Mrs. Martin as she told the tale to her husband. "They said he'd had a shock—an electric shock, to my way of thinking! It was . . . well, you tell him, Jamie."

"I yem Jameth Marriteen int I comf rom Cass-ell-tónn!" yelled Jamie in a voice that was not spot on but as near an imitation as any human could hope to make.

Calypso had been snoozing with her chin on the hearth. At Jamie's words she jumped up and looked round, silent but startled, then collapsed back again and curled herself up into a ball.

"Jamie!" said Mrs. Martin. "Stop that dreadful noise."

Then she turned to her husband and said, "That's nearly what it was like, though. He sounded like the Thing from Outer Space! Jamie says he's lost his memory."

Mr. Martin rummaged down the side of his chair and brought up a newspaper.

"Sounds as if he might be the lad they were on about in yesterday's *Journal.*"

He straightened out the newspaper. There on the bottom left-hand side of the front page was a short item with the headline "Little Boy Lost."

" 'Police are trying to trace the parents of a young boy who was severely traumatized after witnessing the crash on Walgate Hill yesterday lunchtime.' "

"It seems," said Mr. Martin, summarizing the account in his own words, "that the lad's lost his memory. No mention here of a strange voice, though. No photo either. Probably too early for them to know much."

"We'll hear more about it," said his wife. "You'll see if we don't. I know you'll think it's fanciful, but he sounded to me like an alien, an undesirable one at that!"

Jamie heard her condemnation and was silently indignant. Whatever his mother said, the boy in the hospital was good fun, and definitely a friend. Then as the words *outer space* and *alien* hovered in his consciousness, Jamie was visited by another idea, a true Jamesian inspiration.

What if Sammy *was* an alien?

What if the voice *did* belong to another planet?

Organbat, or wherever it was, was not in Africa after all! It could easily be somewhere in outer space! And the boy could be stranded, stranded on the wrong planet, a prisoner of Earth! Jamie's flight of fancy ended with a decision to offer his new friend help.

"I want to send a card to Sammy. I want to give him a present," he said suddenly.

"Sammy?" said his mother.

"The boy in the hospital," said Jamie, "the one who's lost his memory. That was what the nurses called him. He'll be having a rotten Christmas in there by himself."

"Why should you?" said his mother. "You hardly knew him for two minutes."

"I knew him Friday and Saturday," said Jamie vehemently. "I knew him as long as I knew Cousin Josie and you always make me send her a Christmas card. I like him better than I like Cousin Josie. I don't care if I never see Cousin Josie again!"

"All right, all right," said his dad. "Simmer down. If you want to send the lad a card, you can. I'll pop it in the post myself tomorrow morning. How about that?"

"I want to send him a card, and a letter, and a present," said Jamie, looking absolutely stubborn.

"You can't get a present at this time of night," said his dad, which was exactly the wrong thing to say. By explaining that it would not be possible to buy a present there and then, Mr. Martin was conceding that, if only it had been possible, a present might have been bought.

"He can have the model airplane I won at the Mariners' Christmas party. It's still in its wrapper."

"But you like it," said his dad. "You were pleased as punch when you won it."

"Yes, I like it," said Jamie aggressively. "I wouldn't give a friend a present I didn't like, would I?"

With this sort of argument, and playing on his recent scary operation, Jamie got his father to agree to hand the parcel in at the hospital on his way to work next day. It would not be much out of his way, after all. Mr. Martin worked in the Customs House on the quayside.

"Don't put our address on the note," said Jamie's mother as he sat down at the desk to compose his letter. "We don't want him knowing where we live. You can feel sorry for him, but you don't know anything about him—that voice was far from normal and well you know it."

Jamie said nothing. He wrote his letter on a piece of notepaper from a sheaf his Granny Armstrong had given him "for fun." He tucked it inside a Christmas card; then he made up a parcel with the airplane and the card sealed up inside.

"You didn't put our address on it?" Mrs. Martin insisted as he handed over the package to his dad.

"No, I didn't," said Jamie. "You said I couldn't."

And she knew he hadn't. There was no need to check up on him. He was that sort of boy. They were that sort of family.

Chapter 25

At Dead of Night

"Waverley station?" said the taxi driver, confirming the order he'd been given.

"That's right," said Patrick. He put the holdall on the backseat beside him and fastened his seat belt. The journey was short, but at that hour of the night it made more sense to travel by car.

The taxi turned right when it left the square and headed up the back streets, the driver muttering something about "these ruddy one-way streets," though he knew well enough that taxis were not barred from Princes Street at that hour of the morning.

"Didn't know there was a train from Waverley soon as this," he said over his shoulder to his passenger.

"Penzance train," said Patrick, not caring now whether his glib lie would be detected at some later date. "Might not always run, but there's one on tonight, maybe to get people home for Christmas."

"Mmm," said the driver. At that point they came to

the road leading into the station. Patrick got out and paid the fare, then walked as if into the station itself. This was purely to convince the driver.

After waiting awhile in the shadows, Patrick prepared for the next part of his journey. His document case was safe in the poacher's pocket. The trowel in the outer pocket was ready to hand. Only the holdall was an unnecessary encumbrance. He had needed it for the taxi and the hotel, but now it, and everything in it, was totally superfluous. Patrick guiltily tucked it under a bench seat, then hurried out into the street again.

There, across the road, was the monument.

Patrick walked toward it, watching carefully to left and right to make sure that no one was likely to see his next endeavors. He would definitely appear to be acting suspiciously!

Fortunately, the whole of Edinburgh seemed to have gone to sleep. There really is, in any town, something one can call the dead of night. On Princes Street there was hardly a movement; the odd stray car passed by in loneliness, seeking no doubt a warm destination.

Patrick crossed to the gate that led into the park. There he came to a setback he might have foreseen. The gate was locked. A gate almost at shoulder height and surmounted with wicked spikes.

Patrick walked round the corner to the side gate. Being on a slope, it was a little less high, though still a considerable obstacle to anyone wishing to enter the area stealthily.

Still, what had to be done had to be done. Patrick removed his coat and threw it over the gate so that it landed in a heap on the other side. Then he gripped the spikes and pulled himself up near the gate hinge, where there was just a fraction more room for a foothold. Carefully and slowly he got to the point where, crouching over the spikes, he managed to leap forward onto the coat. It was not a perfect landing. His left hand missed the coat altogether and was badly grazed; his knees felt the jolt even through the sheepskin.

He got up gingerly, put on his coat, and hurried across to the beech tree, where he sat on the ground for a few minutes, his back against the tree trunk, recovering.

Then, lying flat on the ground, he approached with all the stealth of a commando the patch of soil where the spaceship was buried. He must not be seen from the street. Fortunately, the place where he needed to dig was well overshadowed by the fence around the monument. Livingstone's statue was another source of protection, not perfect, but better than nothing.

Once he had reached the spot, however, Patrick had no choice but to raise himself up into a near-sitting position in order to use the trowel. Leaning heavily on his left elbow, with his right hand he thrust the trowel's blade as deep as he could diagonally into the earth. Some soil moved. Patrick raked and scraped away at it.

Then he was suddenly aware of light somewhere behind his shoulder. A car passing. Patrick sank to the ground and stayed still.

Darkness.

Try again.

The trowel was sharp, but the soil was difficult. Patrick found he had to use both hands for the task. He dug with the trowel and scraped with his fingers, scratching crumbled soil aside like a dog digging for a bone. And all the time he felt exposed, sitting too high from the ground.

Gradually he got through to damper soil that was more workable. He flung handfuls to either side and used the trowel and both arms to make a wider tunnel into the earth. It was going well. He was getting there. His work took on a rhythm.

Then—

"Wha' ya a-doin' ower theerr?" called a voice from the pavement.

Patrick froze.

"Wha' ya doin, mister?"

Looking toward the road, Patrick saw a little tramp in a bunched-up overcoat peering through the railings. In one hand he held a bottle that bumped with a clatter against the iron rails.

Patrick took the measure of the man, then turned round and went on digging. Any second now he should touch the spaceship and would disappear. Once he was gone, no one would believe the word of a drunken tramp.

"Can ya no' hear, mon?" yelled the tramp.

Now, drunks can have very odd thoughts—and this particular drunk was suddenly visited by the memory of his old granny in wartime warning him against turning a lever in the wall of the air-raid shelter. "If ye di tha', ye'll hae the whole place doon atop of us."

The thought made him hysterical. He had an instant

vision of the mighty monument scattering itself all over Princes Street and burying all around in its debris.

"Ye'll hae to stobbit!" he yelled. "I'm tellin' ye, mister, ye'll hae to stobbit."

At that moment the tunnel Patrick was making began to cave in, as if whatever was inside could take no more of the noise. Patrick stopped digging. After a split second's thought, he ran to the gate that before had defeated him. Then, with superhuman strength born of desperation, he grabbed the gatepost, took a mammoth leap, and landed on his feet in front of the intruder. He looked down at him and again took his measure. This was another Canty, a distinctly unfortunate mortal, but probably more witless than Patrick's old friend.

Patrick glared at him and said sternly, "I am an alien from outer space and I am digging in the soil over there to find my spaceship. It is buried just beside that fence. And I will thank you to let me work in peace."

The tramp gulped and looked up at him, saying anxiously, "No offense, sir. No harrrm done, I'm sure."

Patrick smiled as insanely as he could and added in the strongest Ormingat tones, *"Yiggo, yiggo, Vateelin callantig!"*

The tramp dropped the bottle he'd been holding, and it crashed to the pavement and shattered. Patrick put out one hand to steady him and he drew away, horrified. Then he turned on his heel and ran off with a speed that would not have disgraced him in the hundred meters at Meadowbank.

Patrick watched him go and laughed nervously.

Then, subduing what was after all a sort of hysteria, he leaped over the gate again, using the technique he had learned by now, and went back to the task in hand. This time he sat up straighter and kept his face toward the road. This posture was less comfortable and not so easy for working, but it felt much safer.

Feverishly he scooped out the soil that had fallen back into the hole, dug deeper and deeper with the trowel. The hole widened, the work became easier, as if his power was increasing.

After just five more minutes, it was all over. His fingers touched the sphere beneath the soil, and his whole body shrank into it, as swiftly as if the object below were quenching some great thirst. It was as if the genie were returning to the lamp.

Then the tunnel collapsed and the loose soil was sucked into it.

Dennis Brodie, a tramp of many years' standing (and sitting and lying down), did not stop in his run along Princes Street till he collided with a policeman coming in the opposite direction. The constable barely understood the tale he told of a mad alien searching for a spaceship beneath the scaffolding surrounding the Scott Monument, but he walked back with him to check, and to give a little company to a soul who seemed to need it.

When they came to the spot, the policeman shone his torch through the railings toward the place the tramp indicated. He was surprised to see that there was, in fact, evidence of digging. Soil was scattered onto the path. There was clearly some disturbance. But not much, nothing really significant.

"A dog," said the constable, pocketing his torch again. "A stray, no doubt. You did well to report it. I'll see that it's mentioned." And he tactfully refrained from any reference to the tale he had been told earlier. The little fellow was drunk, that was clear enough.

Stepping further back on the pavement, the policeman noticed the fragments of broken glass scattered there.

"I suppose it wasn't you broke that bottle?" he said in a voice that was quite kindly.

Dennis gave him a look that was murderous, but he said nothing. *Some folk*, he thought, *will never listen.*

In the earth below, Vateelin lay recovering from the trauma of reduction. He had underestimated how long that would take. But at least there was no fear of being found out now. The powerful protection of the ship was all around him as he slept.

Time was the only enemy.

Chapter 26

Six Days to Go

Vateelin lay on a couch in the living quarters of the ship. There was no partition between that and the area where the instruments were, but there was a demarcation of comfort. The living quarters had soft upholstered furnishings and a feeling of human warmth, a midway to Earth. The other half of the sphere was austere and clinical by contrast, more like a laboratory. The only light in the spaceship came as a glow from screens and instruments. That was how it would be till Earth was left behind.

Three hours after his reentry into the ship, Vateelin woke up properly and moved into the work area, hoping to set in motion all that was needful to recover his son. He was still thinking and speaking in English, but that was as meant—debriefing would take all of the three years' journey home.

He bent over the instrument panel and clicked a switch along a horizontal groove and into a loop.

Before the voice of the ship could speak, Vateelin demanded urgently, "Where is my son? Where is Tonitheen?"

A voice replied in an English that sounded somehow off-key to Vateelin's ears.

"You have returned late," it said. "You were expected two days ago."

"But where is my son?" said Vateelin. "Where is Tonitheen?"

"You have returned late," said the machine. "You were expected two days ago."

Vateelin looked despairingly at the greenish glow on the screen in front of him.

He tried rephrasing the question. "Tonitheen, the boy. Have you any trace on his voice?"

"You have returned late," the machine began again, as if there were a scratch on the disc.

Vateelin angrily yanked the switch from its loop and slid it back so that the screen went dull. He had some thoughts of leaving the ship, to search alone for his son and give up all hope of returning to Ormingat. He wished he had defected from the first.

But the scientists of Ormingat were clever. Of this ship, even at this distance of space and time, they were in total control. Vateelin could switch off the voice but he could not command the machine to obey him and he could not leave the ship. Passengers knew no more than they needed to know. It absolved them of responsibility.

After a few moments' thought, Vateelin wearily slid

the switch into the loop again. When in doubt, begin at the beginning.

"I am late," he said. "I should have returned two days ago. There was an accident . . ."

That was the key word, the word the machine was waiting for.

"The accident is recorded," it said. "It was not your fault. You will not be held responsible."

It was a comfort to realize that the machine knew so much, but Vateelin had not managed to get an answer to the most important question.

"I need help," he said.

Once more he had uttered an important key word, the most important one.

"You need help," said the machine. "Look at the clock."

That seemed an irrelevancy, but by now Vateelin had grown calm. Five years away from this machine had made him forget how precise it was, how undeflectable. He obeyed its command and looked down at the clock.

The so-called clock was a large disk set in the floor of the ship. Its face was black, with tiny stars set in it like pinpricks in velvet. Down its center, like a meridian, there was a groove dividing its east from its west. These were the static objects on the disk. Moving across and around it, quite slowly, were ten globules of light.

Five years ago, when Vateelin and Tonitheen left the spaceship, these globules of light, fascinating to both man and boy, had been moving in disparate orbits, each disappearing in different directions and at different times around the back of the disk. Now, four of them were moving in a straight line, one above the other. The fifth was nearing this vertical; the other, not far off, looked like a wavering tail.

"That is the firing mechanism," said the voice. "When all lights come in line they will drop into the groove, the great rocket will detonate, and this ship will start its journey home."

"On the twenty-sixth, Earth time," said Vateelin rapidly. "The calendar was converted, the date was fixed."

"The lights will come in line," said the machine, "six nights from now, at midnight. And in the hours before it is due to leave, the ship will seal and countdown will begin."

"But my son," said Vateelin. "I cannot leave without him."

"There is no override," said the voice. "The ship will leave on time."

Vateelin remembered the word that had worked before.

"Help," he said. "Tonitheen needs help."

"A voice scan has picked up Tonitheen's tones and is locating them precisely, though it would be easier if he had not ceased transmitting."

Those words terrified Vateelin. If Tonitheen had ceased transmitting, why had he done so? What could have happened?

Vateelin looked at the flickering screen and was reduced to using the one word that seemed to provoke any response.

"Help," he said. *"Entesh, Argule, entesh."* For in extremis each being will use his own name for God.

The machine continued in its flat English voice.

"Permission has been sought to take the ship to a point from which the boy can be retrieved."

"Argule, alayis," murmured Vateelin thankfully.

"Permission has not yet been received."

The screen went dark.

"Help," said Vateelin again. "Oh, help."

And at that very moment another globule fell in line.

Chapter 27

Publicity

It was Monday afternoon.

Since the inspector's visit on Saturday, Thomas had been very, very quiet. He ate and slept, moving where and when he was told to move, looking more and more retired into a secret self. The nurses were concerned, of course they were, but there was little they could do. Thomas curled up inside and would not even look at them.

When the inspector came in to see the boy, just after tea that Monday, even he noticed the change. Thomas's stubbornness had become something that looked more and more like a real mental breakdown. He did not seem to be pretending.

"He will stay here over the holiday," said Dr. Ramsay when Inspector Galway inquired about Thomas, "and I have arranged for Dr. Marston to see him early next week. He is our consultant psychiatrist but he's on holiday at the moment."

"I would be a lot happier if we could trace his relatives, whoever they are. He still hasn't been reported missing and that is very strange," said Inspector Galway, "given that he is not some street urchin. His clothes are good and quite expensive. He has obviously been well looked after all his life. So where are his parents? We should go to the media. It's one area where they can be useful."

Dr. Ramsay looked thoughtful.

"That has been discussed. I must admit I am reluctant to do so at present because—well, as you see, the boy is hardly forthcoming. I don't want to submit him to any more traumatic experiences. It's a decision I'd prefer to leave to Dr. Marston."

"How do you know it would be traumatic?" said Inspector Galway quickly. "Do you mind if I ask him? If he agrees, then I don't see any problem."

"He won't answer," said the doctor. "You can see the way he is. It's not worth trying."

"He might give some sign, even if he doesn't speak," said the inspector. "He has responded to me before. He has the right to be given the chance. You don't honestly know what's wrong with him, do you?"

"Well, keep it short," said Dr. Ramsay, thinking that this was one way to end the argument. "But if he is distressed, you must leave off immediately."

Inspector Galway crossed to the bed where Thomas, fully dressed, lay on his side, facing the wall, with his knees drawn almost up to his chin. The inspector sat down on the chair beside him. Dr. Ramsay came close enough to hear what was said. He did not fully trust the visitor's curiosity.

"I know you can hear me," said Inspector Galway, placing one hand lightly on Thomas's arm. "I have a suggestion to make that you might agree to. I won't even ask you to speak. Just nod if you agree—the way you did before."

There was no sign at all that Thomas was listening. The inspector was speaking distinctly and firmly to the back of the boy's head.

"I can get the television people to come here and see you," he said. "They needn't even speak to you. I'll do all the talking. But someone out there might be looking in, see your face, and know who you are. Someone out there might come forward and put everything straight. How about it?"

Thomas turned slowly to face his visitor. His eyes were red with crying. He spoke in his own English voice for the first time.

"Do what you want," he said listlessly.

Inspector Galway started. He had not really expected Thomas to speak. Dr. Ramsay, standing behind the inspector, prodded him quite hard on the shoulder, warning him not to comment, not to press it any further. To him it was good news that the boy could speak in a natural voice, but his experience of sick and traumatized children told him not to push it. One step forward can so easily be followed by two steps back.

* * *

A reporter with a camera team turned up two hours later. His interest in the boy was not very great, but he had heard of the mysterious missing crash victim and had been promised an interview with the tanker driver and his mate.

The interview with the boy took place first, in a little waiting room off the main ward. Thomas sat in a children's armchair and Inspector Galway stood beside him with one hand proprietarily on the chair back.

"And you say this boy has never spoken since the crash?" said the reporter after an introduction in which the viewers were shown shots of the crash site with the huge tanker piled onto the little red post office van. The reporter, Gerry Potterton, was young and eager and hoped to get beyond the local news he still covered.

"Not exactly," said the inspector cautiously. "But he is very, very reluctant to speak."

Next, the jacket Thomas was wearing when found was shown to the camera. Then the things that were found in the pocket: a travel Scrabble, and a keyring with a plastic rocket for a fob.

The camera then zoomed in on Thomas's face. Suddenly confronted with the camera and all the attention he was being given, Thomas felt inspired. His father had told him to say the Ormingat names to no one, except in the direst of circumstances. It followed, then, that if the direst of circumstances should come, saying the names, using the keys, would have to be a very public pronouncement. It was scientific! It was not mumbo jumbo after all! It was some form of broadcasting. The names were meant to be picked up by someone from his own planet. It was so obvious he could not understand why he had not realized it before. It was his one link to his father, his one chance of making contact.

"Vateelin Tonitheen Ormingat," he said loudly.

And in thousands of homes in the northern region, sound appeared on vision, zigzagging across the screen. The interviewer, the cameraman, and the inspector jumped back, bewildered.

"Ormingat Vateelin Tonitheen," said the boy in an even louder voice, so that the zigzags on everybody's screen went wild. In the studio they blamed this weird effect on the atmospherics that the outside broadcast had produced. In the waiting room, all who were there shivered at the sound. It was Gerry Potterton who recovered first.

"The boy has spoken!" he said in a voice full of genuine excitement. "But this is a voice such as we have never heard before. Heaven alone knows what our sound engineers are making of *this*! I don't know what it is doing to our listeners out there, but here in this hospital room, it has set the blood curdling. Where are you from, boy? What do you *know*?"

The reporter bent eagerly toward Thomas, thrusting the microphone in front of him.

Inspector Galway motioned him to stay further back.

Dr. Ramsay took the more drastic action of sweeping aside the hand that held the microphone and saying, "That is enough, *quite* enough for now. This child is ill.

174

If any of your viewers can identify him, I would ask them to come forward as soon as possible."

The look on the doctor's face was sufficient to prevent further harassment.

Gerry signaled to the studio that this part of the interview was over. A break was needed to give him time to get to the ward upstairs.

The studio cut to the picture of the crash scene once again and to another reporter's description of how a strip of sheepskin was the only clue to a most bizarre mystery.

Then it was back to the live outside broadcast again. By this time Gerry had reached the men's ward on the top floor. In one bed, Andy Brown was lying with his left arm and shoulder all swathed in bandages. In the bed next to him, Jack Jordan had a plastered leg held up on a sling. Both were ready and eager to speak.

"And next," said Gerry, "we shall address the problem of the missing body, the tale, as it were, of the sheepskin coat!"

Other patients in the ward were straining forward to observe this interesting diversion from the normal dull routine. Fancy the telly being there!

"So, what do *you* think happened, Andy?" said Gerry after the preliminaries had been got out of the way.

Andy Brown looked like anybody's grandfather: thinning gray hair, leathery face, a big nose and little, sharp eyes.

"I don't *think*," he said impatiently. "I *know*. If

there's not a man dead under the wheels of the tanker, it's a ruddy miracle. We saw 'im with our own eyes. Didn't we, Jack?''

He turned to the man in the next bed for confirmation. Except that the nose was smaller and the eyes were larger and watery blue, he bore exactly the same stamp as his friend and fellow worker.

"That's right," he said. "He was walking across the crossing, lad running in front of him. We knew what was happening and there wasn't a danged thing we could do."

"Of course, the full cause of the crash has not yet been ascertained," said Gerry, smiling, "but for the moment, the real interest lies in this strip of sheepskin."

He held the strip up for the camera to see.

"Two inches wide, about eighteen inches long," he said. "Or if you prefer, four centimeters, give or take, by half a meter. And this was found clinging to the tanker's front wheel, freshly torn from a coat such as these men say the crash victim was wearing. Well, what do you think, folks? What happened to the man in the crossing? Why has no body been found? A miraculous escape, perhaps? A touch of the supernatural? We'll keep you posted. And if there's someone out there missing a strip from his sheepskin coat, do us a favor, mate—get in touch!"

To end the broadcast, the news reader in the studio gave out a telephone number for anyone to call with information about the nameless boy or the missing "victim."

Chapter 28

A Buzz in Belthorp

"There she is, Mam, just goin' into her gate. Come on, come on, let's see if she knows," said Mickey Trent, tugging his mother by the arm and pulling her in the direction of the Merrivale cottages. They had just got off the bus from Hartwell. Mrs. Trent was carrying two bags full of Christmas shopping. Her son gave up on the effort to make her hurry and sped off down the street, calling Mrs. Dalrymple's name.

Stella was carrying a stack of parcels piled as high as her chin. She turned to see what the noise was about and Mickey bumped right into her.

"Whoa!" she said with a smile. "Not so fast. This is a built-up area!"

She clutched the parcels to save them from falling. It was the day of the church bazaar and Stella was acting as factotum in the absence of several parishioners who, for one reason or another, were not able to help. So, in every sense, she had her hands full.

"Sorry about that, Mrs. Dalrymple," said Mickey's mother as she caught up with him. "He's just excited about seeing Thomas on the news last night—and worried too, of course. We all are."

Stella looked at them blankly. She had not seen last night's news.

"He's in the hospital in Casselton, Mrs. Dalrymple," said Mickey, in a rush to tell the story first, "and he doesn't know who he is."

Stella looked at Mrs. Trent for an explanation. When it was given, she was more worried than anyone else in the village would have been. Everyone knew, of course, how close she was to the Derwents. They had long been spoken of as "Mrs. Dalrymple's neighbors."

"Are you sure it was Thomas?" she said. "His father was with him. They were on the way to London to board a plane to Canada. You *must* be mistaken."

"It'll be on the lunchtime news," said Jenny Trent. "They always repeat things. Why don't you go in and watch it? It'll be on any minute now."

All three of them went into Stella's house, put down the parcels and the shopping, then went into the little sitting room to wait for the regional news. Sure enough, the item of the night before was repeated, though in an abbreviated form. The sound engineers must not have been able to cope with the distortion caused by Thomas's alien voice. But there he was, a boy with no name, in Casselton General Hospital.

"That's the keyring I gave him," said Mickey. He was glad that the sounds Thomas had made were omitted. One of those sounds was too close to a whisper he had heard; one of those sounds was a word that he and he alone could recognize. He had no idea what it might mean, but it was a secret he would never tell.

Stella gasped. "I gave him the Scrabble," she said. "That *is* Thomas. Dear God, what on earth's happened to him? And where is Patrick?"

With a feeling of horror, she saw the strip of sheepskin and wondered what *could* have happened to the two people for whom she cared so much. She knew that Patrick had been wearing a sheepskin coat. It was, at the very least, a chilling coincidence.

The first thing to do was to telephone the number given in the program. The other two sat and watched, Mrs. Trent feeling guilty that she had not done so herself.

Jenny Trent needn't have worried. There had already been dozens of phone calls from all sorts of people claiming to know the lost boy. The names given for him were wide-ranging; the localities were many and varied.

"Cranks," Sergeant Morland said with a sigh. "Cranks, knaves, and sad people!"

But they all had to be checked.

"This is interesting, though," said the sergeant as he looked down the list he had meticulously made, in strict alphabetical order, together with the time of the call, the number—where obtainable—of the caller, and the location of the boy's potential home.

Mrs. Dalrymple had just identified Thomas Derwent.

And there on the sergeant's list was the name Thomas Derwent, given by someone called Sam Swanson, who said that his son had recognized a schoolmate on the news.

"Can you give us more details, Mrs. Dalrymple?" he said. Then he pressed on rapidly with a barrage of questions.

Stella answered all the sergeant's queries—about the boy, his father, their destination, and numerous other details that seemed irrelevant and sometimes totally meaningless. Sammy Bentley? Strange voices?

Eventually Stella cut across all this and said firmly, "I am coming to see Thomas myself. It can't be this afternoon because I have promised to help with the Christmas bazaar and there are already too few helpers to go round. But this evening—"

"It is a hospital, Mrs. Dalrymple," said Sergeant Morland. "Evening visits on a children's ward are not permitted. You will have to wait till tomorrow."

"I can't come in the morning," said Stella, irritated by another delay she could not avoid. "It's the last day at work before the Christmas break but I shall certainly be there tomorrow afternoon. In the meantime, I shall ring the hospital."

"Yes?" said the sergeant, not quite sure what Stella meant to do.

"You have asked me a lot of questions, Sergeant Morland," she said tartly, "but you have not told me how Thomas is. The amnesia diagnosis was fairly obvious, but is he physically injured in any way? Have they checked properly? Are they sure that there is no concussion?"

Mrs. Trent winced. *She* had been too timid even to ring the number. And here was Stella Dalrymple trying to put them all in their places!

"I think you'll find, Mrs. Dalrymple," said Sergeant Morland, "that everything that should be done has been done. But do feel free to ring the children's ward and inquire. Tell them you have spoken to me."

"And what about the boy's father?" said Stella. "Have you no idea where he might be?"

"Not yet," said Sergeant Morland grittily. "But we are working on it."

He was still not a hundred percent sure that the boy *was* Thomas Derwent. But at least Inspector Galway would be happy to have something to go on.

"Can I come with you to see Thomas, Mrs. Dalrymple?" said Mickey after the phoning was over. "He'll talk to me. I know he will."

His mother frowned at him.

"Don't be so forward, Mickey. Mrs. Dalrymple won't want to take a child with her when she visits the hospital. And it's a long way to go."

Stella looked from Mickey to his mother, considered quickly, then said, "If you've no objection, Mrs. Trent, I would like him to come with me. He and Thomas are such good friends. It might be a help."

181

Chapter 29

Visiting Time

On Wednesday morning Dr. Ramsay came to see Thomas.

He sat down on the chair next to the bed, crossed his legs, and perched a clipboard on his knee. He was holding a pen in one hand and scanning a page of writing.

"Well now," he said. "We are just about sure that you are not called Sammy Bentley. So much you have confirmed yourself."

Thomas did not look at him and tried hard to appear not to be listening. His face was as near a mask as he could make it. Patrick had not come for him and the waiting was becoming harder and harder.

I have done all I can, he thought. *I can do no more.*

Except wait, he told himself sharply, *just wait. Another day, another night, maybe. Like going twice round the moon.* Late did not mean never.

Dr. Ramsay looked up from the page and said

sharply, hoping to surprise the boy into some sort of normal reaction, "We are almost certain that you are called Thomas Derwent and that you come from Belthorp."

That *was* a shock. It was the last thing Thomas had expected him to say. He longed to ask how he knew. His mind skimmed the possibilities and came up with the right answer. Stella must have seen the news and recognized him. To be on television had been yet another mistake. It had not brought his father any nearer; it had let people know who he was and where he came from. That could be dangerous.

"Well, Thomas, what have you to say to that? Nod if you like. I don't need you to speak," said the doctor. But somehow Dr. Ramsay had not the same authority in his tone as Inspector Galway. The inspector's style combined strength with nonchalance in a way that reached Thomas; perhaps the manner somehow resembled that of his father. Whatever the reason, Thomas was not prepared to make similar concessions to the doctor. He continued stony-faced and silent.

"You are to have a visitor this afternoon," said Dr. Ramsay, telling more than he should have told on this occasion, depriving himself of the chance of taking Thomas by surprise again. "Mrs. Dalrymple, your next-door neighbor, is coming all the way from Belthorp to see you."

 On the train to Casselton, neither Mickey nor Stella had very much to say. Each was wrapped in

183

thought. Stella was longing for the journey to be over so that she could solve the mystery and begin to put things right. Mickey was wondering whether to mention something he knew and Mrs. Dalrymple didn't.

"He spoke," said Mickey at length as the train was nearing Casselton.

"Who do you mean?" said Stella. "Thomas?"

"On the telly, the bit they missed out when you saw it," said Mickey, puzzling what to say next. "He spoke in a shivery voice and the picture went funny."

"What did he say?" said Stella anxiously.

"I don't know," said Mickey. "It was like foreign and . . . and . . . shivery."

It was the first inkling Stella had that this mission might not be perfectly straightforward.

When they reached the hospital, they were shown into an office where Dr. Ramsay was already waiting. He was surprised and annoyed to see the child.

"I thought you would be coming alone," he said, looking sternly at Mrs. Dalrymple. "I have not prepared my patient to receive two visitors."

Mrs. Dalrymple smiled, recognizing in the doctor a man who was caring but probably overcautious.

"Mickey is Thomas's best friend," she said. "I thought it might help him to see more than one familiar face. If he is suffering from amnesia, as you say he is, then surely anything that might jog his memory should be helpful."

Dr. Ramsay was worried. He knew how difficult his patient had been. There was, besides, the business of the voice that had in it a pitch that might be madness. And was the boy really Thomas Derwent after all?

"I think you should go in first, Mrs. Dalrymple. Make your own assessment. Mickey can stay here with me," he said, trying to signal that Mickey might be upset to see Thomas in his present state, especially if he really was so close to him. The whole business seemed to be getting out of hand. The sooner the boy was seen by Mattie Marston, the better.

"Very well," said Mrs. Dalrymple. "That seems fair enough."

Dr. Ramsay went to the doorway and called to Kirsty Mackenzie, "Would you please take this visitor to see the child we've been calling Sammy?"

He followed Mrs. Dalrymple out into the corridor and closed the door behind him so that Mickey could not hear.

"You may see the boy alone," he said softly, "but call the nurse immediately if he becomes distressed. In any event, keep your visit brief. Don't mention his father. And don't say anything about the crash or the strip of sheepskin. Ten minutes should be enough at first. Then come back here and see me."

Mrs. Dalrymple made no protest. She had other ideas, but it was unnecessary to discuss them yet. She followed Kirsty down the corridor.

She saw Thomas as soon as she entered the ward, though his bed was in the furthest corner, just beneath the window. She waved and walked toward him. He was lying on top of his covers, propped up by pillows, hands flanking his sides. He was wearing the same jeans and sweatshirt that he had worn on the day he left Belthorp.

"Well, Thomas," said Stella as she sat down in the bedside chair, "are you pleased to see me?"

The boy's face was blank and he looked fixedly ahead of him. Stella suddenly understood why Dr. Ramsay was so worried. She leaned forward and grasped the child's hand but it stayed limp in hers. She said no more for some seconds and just held on to his hand. It was like being with someone in a trance. She racked her brains for some way of snapping him out of it, some gentle, harmless way.

"The decorations are nice," she said at length, looking up at the hoops hanging from the ceiling. "I've got my little Christmas tree out again. I wasn't going to bother now that you aren't there, but then I thought, why not? It is not only children who enjoy the brightness of Christmas."

Thomas squirmed. He was puzzled by Stella's apparent lack of reaction to his silence. He began very deliberately to say the twelve-times table inside his head.

"I practically ran the church bazaar myself yesterday," she said. "It's funny how people find excuses to shy away from work. Still, it was worth it. We had plenty of customers and our takings were well up on last year. I even managed to sell that old fur coat Mrs. Bigwood gave us."

Thomas was tempted to smile at the thought of Rosie's mother's huge fur coat. The other children had unkindly called her Yogi Bear. He wanted to ask who

186

bought it. In another world, another time, he would have. His eyes for a moment slid from a blank frontal stare to a quick glance in Stella's direction. *Nine twelves are a hundred and eight.*

"Come on, Thomas, look at me," said Stella, seeing the glance immediately and knowing exactly what it meant. "Look me straight in the eye. Whatever is wrong can't be put right while you're lying here. I'll see to it. Have I ever let you down? If you speak to me now, I shall take on the whole hospital on your behalf and I will get you home to Belthorp. That is a promise."

Twelve twelves are a hundred and forty-four.

Stella kept to the rules—no mention of Patrick, no mention of the crash, and certainly no mention of the sheepskin coat. But the promise she had made covered everything. Thomas was greatly tempted. Perhaps, perhaps, he thought, Stella could find Vateelin—but then he realized with a shock that he no longer thought of his father as Patrick. The Belthorp part of their existence had slipped away. It was a sadness, but it was inevitable. *Vateelin is not Patrick; and I, I am not Thomas Derwent.*

He let his hand stay limp. He fixed his gaze on a point in front of him and refused to move it again. *Four elevens are forty-four. Four elevens are forty-four. Four elevens are forty-four. . . .*

Five elevens . . . five elevens are fifty-five. Six elevens are sixty-six. Seven elevens . . .

The refusal to look her way, the marble immobility of the boy's face, persisted. Stella found herself unnerved by it, worried that any further effort she might make could make things worse. Thomas might be shamming amnesia, but his illness could still be something real.

A nurse came behind her and gently put one hand on the visitor's shoulder.

"Dr. Ramsay would like to see you now," she said quietly.

"You do see what I mean?" said Dr. Ramsay when Stella returned to the office. Mickey sat there puzzled and silent. "It would not be good for Mickey to see him today. We've been having quite a chat, Mickey and I. He'd like to come back again when Thomas feels well enough to see him."

"What is wrong with him?" Stella demanded, cutting across the doctor's diplomatic kindliness.

"Take Mickey down to the dayroom, please," said Dr. Ramsay to Kirsty. "I'm sure you can find something interesting for him to look at while Mrs. Dalrymple and I have a little talk.

"I'll try to explain," said Dr. Ramsay after Mickey left. "Thomas is not physically ill. And though it might look alarming, the state he is in now will not persist. It is most probably nothing more than the aftereffects of shock, but people often underestimate how devastating shock can be."

Stella studied carefully what to say next. Shock to her was something treated with a cup of warm, sweet tea in the comfort of one's own home.

"Let me take him back to Belthorp, then," she said. "It could be what he needs."

"Impossible," said Dr. Ramsay. "Have you not understood me? He needs professional medical attention. I would be in dereliction of my duty to let him go."

"I'm not saying I'll remove him from proper care," said Stella quickly. "There's Dr. Page in the village, and I'd get Nurse Harvey to pop in. We're a very close, caring community."

"Give it another day or two," said Dr. Ramsay. "We honestly can't make any drastic decisions at this stage. Do remember, the police still have a strong interest in the case. There is no next of kin to consult, and however close you might be, you are not the boy's guardian."

"I could be," said Mrs. Dalrymple very deliberately. "I'm sure it could be arranged. I'll come again tomorrow. And in the meantime I shall be seeking advice on ways of getting Thomas back to Belthorp. I mean to have him released into my care in time for Christmas."

Dr. Ramsay was startled. Just as Mrs. Dalrymple had recognized the caring, overcautious doctor, so he saw in Mrs. Dalrymple a woman of fixed purpose for whom rules were often bent and sometimes broken.

"That won't be possible," he said. "We cannot hand patients over to just anybody."

"I am not just anybody," said Mrs. Dalrymple, "and I intend to prove it. My next appointment is with Inspector Galway. I have brought all the evidence I need to prove that the boy in there is who I say he is and that I am the proper person to care for him."

189

* * *

"Was it really Thomas?" said Mickey as he and Mrs. Dalrymple walked down the corridor that led to the outer doors. He was angry at not being allowed to see his friend, an explosive anger hidden behind a scowl.

Stella looked down at him and said resolutely, "It most certainly was, and he won't be staying there for long. That I can tell you!"

"So why couldn't I see him?" said Mickey sharply. "He's my friend and I want to see him. I came here specially."

"I thought it best not to argue too much," said Stella. "There are more important things to argue about. We must make arrangements to get Thomas back to Belthorp."

"Today?" said Mickey.

"Not today," said Stella, "but tomorrow. Certainly tomorrow."

"We'll have to," said Mickey. "It'll be Christmas Eve tomorrow. We can't leave him there for Christmas! Can I come with you again? I'll help you to bring Thomas home. If he needs a wheelchair, I'll push it."

Stella smiled. "He won't need to be wheeled out," she said. "He's quite capable of walking to a taxi and getting onto a train."

At those words, Mickey turned to go back along the corridor. "I'm going to get him," he said. "I'm going to get him now."

"No, Mickey, not yet," said Stella. "That would only make trouble for all of us. We'll have to hurry. We're supposed to be seeing Inspector Galway in less than half an hour.''

But by this time, Mickey was halfway down the corridor, heading for the double doors that led into the children's ward.

Chapter 30

Secrets

The double doors opened just wide enough to admit one small boy.

Mickey, having run the length of the corridor and left Mrs. Dalrymple standing startled, was astute enough to make a quiet entry into the ward. He stood unobserved with his back to the door as he let it close it behind him. He took a quick but thorough look around.

Thick curtains, patterned with brightly colored cars, trains, and airplanes, were drawn round three of the beds: younger children having their afternoon nap. At two other beds, visitors in outdoor clothes were sitting talking quietly to their children. A male nurse was sitting at the desk working, his eyes on the papers in front of him. Another nurse with her back to him had a young child on her knee. And in the far corner, propped up on pillows and lying very still, was Thomas Derwent. Mickey was pleased to note that he was fully dressed. It would have been much more difficult to do what he planned if Thomas had been in pajamas.

Mickey quickly figured out a way to the bed without passing the man at the desk. He would just tiptoe behind his chair and keep close to the wall till he reached the window. Then down by the window to the bed. He hoped Thomas would have the sense not to cry out. Traveling very cautiously, he kept his eyes riveted on the bed where his friend was lying.

Just as he reached the foot of the bed, unbeknownst to him, several things happened at once. Ernie looked up from his papers and glimpsed a boy who looked as if he shouldn't be there. The doors opened again, this time quite wide, and Dr. Ramsay and Mrs. Dalrymple came hurrying in together. Ernie was about to call out to the intruder when Dr. Ramsay waved his arms to signal silence.

The damage was done, the boy was at the bed, and the doctor decided in that split second that they had better wait and see what would happen when the two children came face-to-face. A less cautious man might already have engineered this; now that it had happened, the careful, cautious doctor thought it might not be such a bad idea after all.

Mickey was totally unaware of what was happening behind him. He crept right up to the bed and whispered urgently to Thomas, "I've come to take you home. We can just sneak out. Nobody will notice. There are visitors in the ward, people are busy."

Thomas looked straight at him, but it was a look of desperation.

"Close the curtain," he whispered. "Quickly."

Mickey put one hand behind him and flicked the curtain so that it covered his back. A more elaborate action might, he thought, be too easily noticed. He sat down on the chair by Thomas's bed and leaned forward to talk to him.

Neither boy knew that they were being very discreetly observed.

Thomas reached out a hand, grabbed Mickey's sleeve, and drew him closer toward him.

"I can't leave here," he whispered. "I have to wait for my father."

Mickey looked at him, worried. He knew now just how far Thomas had been shamming, and why. It was the why that was so worrying.

"Your father might not know you are here," he said.

"You know I'm here," said Thomas, his eyes a deeper brown than ever. "Stella knows I am here."

"We saw you on the telly," said Mickey. "Everybody did."

"So my father must have too," said Thomas. "That's why I have to stay here. This is where I spoke from and said the special words. So this is where he'll come to find me. Then we'll go to the spaceship like we're meant to, and we'll travel back to where we belong. Because we don't belong here, you know, Mickey. I wish we did, but we don't. I've always really known that we didn't."

His face was tense but his tone was adamant.

Mickey didn't know what to say, but something had to be said. It wasn't fair to let Thomas think his dad would come for him just like that. As of old, he did not question the spaceship story. But neither did he believe it.

"Nobody knows where your dad is, Thomas," he said. "He might not be able to come for you. Something might have happened to him. I'm not saying it has, but it might have."

"Nothing has happened to my father," said Thomas sharply. "Nothing could ever happen to him."

"Things do happen to people," said Mickey, trying desperately not to say what he really thought. He wondered how much Thomas knew about the crash and the strange disappearance of the man in the sheepskin coat.

"Nothing has happened to my father," said Thomas with a catch in his voice. "You're trying to say my father's dead and he's not. He can't be."

Mickey blushed bright red.

Thomas looked at him wildly and knew that this was what his friend was thinking. He lay back and cried.

"My father is not dead," he said between sobs, and then, in an even lower voice, he murmured feverishly, *"Vateelin, Vateelin, Vateelin, Vateelin mesht."*

Mickey heard him and began to sneeze violently.

✻ Dr. Ramsay and Mrs. Dalrymple were standing by the table where Ernie was still seated. All three were anxiously watching the curtain that hid the two boys. The murmur of voices seemed promising and they glanced at one another hopefully.

Then came what sounded like scuffling and a very loud sneeze.

 Both boys heard the footsteps coming toward the curtain.

Thomas started forward from his pillow and rubbed his eyes vigorously to get rid of the tears.

"Tell no one what I've told you, no one," he said, briefly grasping Mickey's hand. "Promise."

"I promise," said Mickey. "I do promise."

At that moment the curtain was drawn back and Dr. Ramsay was standing there looking down at them. Behind him were Ernie and Mrs. Dalrymple.

Thomas closed his eyes tightly and shut them all out. Dr. Ramsay looked at him, was about to say something, and then thought better of it. He turned toward Mickey instead.

"Well now, what did your chum have to say to you, young Mickey?" he said in the voice he kept for talking to children.

"Nothing," said Mickey sulkily in the voice he kept for talking to grown-ups he did not much like.

"You were talking to each other," said Mrs. Dalrymple in her usual direct way. "We heard you. We couldn't hear what you were saying, but you were certainly saying something."

"I was talking to him, Mrs. Dalrymple," said Mickey. "All he did was make funny noises, a bit like on the telly."

Stella would have gone closer to the bed but Dr.

Ramsay ushered her away. The boy on the bed seemed to be in a deep sleep.

Dr. Ramsay had tea brought to the office and he talked quite gently to Mrs. Dalrymple, as if she were one of his patients. He explained again the need for caution.

"I am sure you believe every word you say," said Stella. "But I am more than ever convinced that this is the wrong place for Thomas. If he were at home with me, sitting by the fire, surrounded by familiar things, I feel sure I could help him get over what you yourself have said is no more than some form of shock."

"You didn't get far with him today," the doctor pointed out.

"I was nervous," said Stella. "A hospital's not a relaxed sort of place. I'm wishing even now that I had had the sense and courage just to cuddle him."

She looked down at her watch, stood up abruptly, and said, "We'll have to be going now. My appointment with Inspector Galway. Come along, Mickey. We'll be back. Have no fear of that."

It was an odd phrase to use. Dr. Ramsay had every fear that this visitor would indeed be back, back and making difficulties.

Chapter 31

Who Is
Thomas Derwent?

Inspector Galway politely examined all the proofs that Stella set before him—from photographs of Thomas taken at his last birthday party, blowing out eleven candles on his cake, to the receipt for the Scrabble game she had bought at Hamley's in Casselton.

In a chair by the door, Mickey sat apart and bemused. It was all much more complicated than he had anticipated.

The inspector looked up from his survey of the "evidence." On the other side of the large desk Stella was waiting, expecting anything except the words that Inspector Galway uttered next.

"We have no doubt at all, Mrs. Dalrymple," he said, "that the child in the hospital is the boy known as Thomas Derwent from the village of Belthorp. But who is Thomas Derwent? Who is Patrick Derwent?"

Stella gave him a look of total incomprehension.

"What do you mean?" she said. "I don't understand you."

The inspector leaned forward with his elbows on the desk, covering the pictures and the other pieces of paper, which included two swimming certificates and a school report.

"We have followed up all the information you gave us on the telephone—we are anxious to talk to Patrick Derwent, obviously. But the information leads nowhere. Patrick Derwent is not employed in any capacity by the Chemicals Complex. Never has been. They have never heard of him."

"I could have been wrong about that," said Stella anxiously. "One assumes things sometimes, without question. Patrick never talked about his work."

"There is no trace of a Patrick Derwent of Belthorp at the Inland Revenue. He does not appear to be paying National Insurance. He has not applied for a passport and he has not booked a passage to Canada. The only evidence we have been able to find of his existence is the fact that he is on the Belthorp electoral register."

Stella hardly knew what to say for the best.

"I don't know what you think that proves," she said coldly, "except perhaps that your searches have not been sufficiently exhaustive. *I* know that Patrick Derwent exists and that he is not the sort of person to live outside the law. You appear to be implying that he is some sort of criminal. Nothing, I do assure you, could be further from the truth."

Inspector Galway bit his lip and sighed. He liked Mrs. Dalrymple; his first impression of her was that she was a strong-willed, good-natured woman not given to nonsense. Whatever she said deserved to be taken seriously.

"You could be right," he said. "I don't defend the system as infallible. It takes a long time to prove a negative. Had Mr. Derwent a driving license?"

"I don't know," said Stella. "He didn't have a car. He relied on trains, buses, and taxis, as most of us do in Belthorp."

"There is one other matter," said the inspector. "You gave Thomas's birthday as November sixteenth."

"Yes?" said Stella, wondering where this could be leading.

"And that he is eleven years old," said the inspector, "which pinpoints for us the boy's date of birth."

"Yes," said Stella, still not sure what the inspector was driving at.

"We have checked," he said. "There is no child of that name registered for that particular date, nor for any of the days within two weeks either side."

"I don't know where he was born," said Stella. "Perhaps he is registered abroad. His father did work for an international company."

"But not the Chemicals Complex," the inspector reminded her. "I know you mean well, Mrs. Dalrymple. That couldn't be clearer. But I'm afraid that, when it comes down to it, you know very little about your neighbors."

Mickey had sat listening and trying to follow what

was being said, and suddenly a totally incredible thought came to him. For the first time ever he began to wonder if Thomas could possibly be telling the truth. The thought was like a thunderbolt.

Mickey looked at the grown-ups, heard the policeman almost accuse the Derwents of some sort of crime. Whatever the truth was, it seemed to Mickey that his friend needed to be defended. So he decided to join in the defense.

"I know Thomas Derwent," he said. "He is my friend and he has been my friend for five years. His father is a good person and so is he."

The inspector turned his full attention on Mickey.

"There are things you don't understand, son," he said, "things nobody expects you to understand. Thomas will be all right. Don't you worry about him."

He pressed the intercom on his desk and asked for a WPC.

"Now, Mickey," he said when the policewoman came in, "you go with WPC Kennedy. Her name's Moira. She'll look after you while Mrs. Dalrymple and I get everything sorted out."

"I have nothing more I can tell you," said Stella after she and the inspector were left alone. "All I need to know now is if *you* can authorize the hospital to release Thomas Derwent into my care."

"I can't do that, Mrs. Dalrymple," said the inspector. "It's not within my province."

At that point Stella's patience gave out.

"Whose province, then?" she said. "Tell me that. There's a frightened and lonely little boy lying bewildered in a hospital ward and all you can do is check for birth certificates and driving licenses and income tax forms. Do people not matter anymore? Do *children* not matter?''

Inspector Galway did not reply in kind. He was quiet and considerate. He rang through on the intercom for a pot of tea.

"Please," he said, "try to consider things a bit more objectively, Mrs. Dalrymple. You have had a few shocks yourself these last two days. There are rules and regulations. Sometimes I don't like them any better than you do. But I have to manage to live with them.''

Stella felt embarrassed at her outburst but still justified in principle.

"Very well," she said more calmly. "What I am asking is very simple. I want to take Thomas home with me and try to patch up Christmas for him. It won't be much. His father is a missing person—I hope you realize that—and Thomas is in a state of shock. But I believe I can do more for him than anyone else. He has been family to me for the past five years. That has to count for something.''

The inspector poured tea into their cups and established that his guest took milk but no sugar. All the while he was considering ways in which he could help.

"This is what I will do," he said at length. "I don't know whether it will be of any use, but we can hope. I will contact the Social Services, I will back your application to foster the boy at least over the holiday period, and I will make sure that Dr. Ramsay knows that you are a fit and proper person. That's the most I can manage. I have no authority over the hospital. Ultimately it will be up to them."

Stella sipped her tea abstractedly.

"With the best will in the world, all this will take time," said the inspector. "Can I suggest you return to the hospital tomorrow afternoon to find out what has been decided? Or perhaps you could ring first—save you a journey if the answer's negative."

"No," said Stella, smiling wanly. "I will come, even if it is only to *see* Thomas."

She got up from her seat and said, "I do appreciate your understanding. By tomorrow, who knows, we might all have some answers. If only you could find Patrick!"

When Stella and Mickey left the police station it was damp and dark, city lights gleaming and city people hastening by under their umbrellas.

Mickey put his hands deep in his pockets and trudged along beside Mrs. Dalrymple, thinking the most astonishing thoughts. Thomas and his father were *not* on their way to Canada. They had *never* been on their way to Canada. Perhaps—*whew*—they really had been going to find that spaceship Thomas talked about! He stole a glance sideways at Mrs. Dalrymple and wondered what he could say to her without breaking his word.

As they crossed by the traffic lights at the foot of Walgate Hill, they both looked up, curious, toward the site of the crash. There was, of course, no sign of it now. The street was as busy as ever.

They walked along in silence, each pursuing private thoughts. Stella was racking her brains in an effort to remember things, to recall anything, *anything*, that might contain a clue. They were nearing the stone portico in front of the railway station when she thought of asking Mickey about Thomas's past. She tried hard to make the question sound casual, conversational.

"Did Thomas ever tell you anything about where he lived before he came to Belthorp?" she said.

Mickey reddened but resolved to speak. It really was too difficult an idea to keep entirely to himself.

"He only ever told me about living in a spaceship and going round the moon. He told me that his dad and him were going back into outer space because that was where they came from."

He hesitated and then added, "Do you think it might be true?"

"That's just like Thomas!" said Stella with a smile and a catch in her voice. "He has always had a very vivid imagination. In any event, he's not going anywhere just now."

"But he *was*," said Mickey, growing braver and less fearful of being mocked. "Everybody knows he was going *somewhere*. And something has happened to stop him."

"There I agree with you," said Stella. "That is why I am going to do all in my power to get him home to Belthorp. Don't you worry about that!"

Mickey gave up. What was the use? People didn't listen.

Chapter 32

What Mickey Knew

Mickey hardly spoke on the train going home. Stella gave him the window seat and a packet of gum she bought in Casselton station. He'd said no thank you to her offer of a comic or a magazine. It was not that he felt shy, or even too tired. He just had a lot to think about.

The train lurched to a halt outside Chamfort station and the passengers were promised half an hour's delay. Mickey's concern for his own mother at once took precedence over his thoughts about Thomas. His mother knew, of course, the train they were coming on. Stella had rung from Casselton especially to set her mind at rest, and to tell her what time they would arrive.

"Will your mother be worried?" said Stella anxiously, seeing how drawn the boy looked.

"If she is, she'll ring the station to ask why the train's late and what time it's expected. She always did that when . . . ," said Mickey, starting a sentence he decided not to finish. He was not going to talk about his dad to a stranger. So he shrugged instead and looked out of the window into darkness.

His mam *would* be worried, even after she rang the station. His mam always worried. It was no use telling her not to—she couldn't help it. Like thinking he had flu every time he sneezed, though the doctor had told her that it was just some sort of allergy and he would probably grow out of it.

Mickey was strong and healthy and much more down-to-earth than his mother. But he respected her nervousness. Like the child in the poem, he always "took good care of his mother." So it was a relief to get home at last and put her mind at rest.

They found her waiting on the doorstep, looking out into the darkness.

"Come in," she said to Mrs. Dalrymple. "Do come in. I've just got the kettle on. I heard the train was late. A stolen car left on the line just outside Chamfort, they said. Lucky there wasn't an accident. I don't know what the world's coming to."

"I hope you haven't been worrying too much," said Mrs. Dalrymple guiltily. It was clear to her that Mickey's mother had been *very* worried.

"No," said Mrs. Trent with an effort. "I knew he'd be safe with you. Still, it's nice that you're both home again. I never did like Casselton. It's a den of thieves and pickpockets. I've read about people there being mugged in broad daylight! You can't open the papers without learning about some crime or other."

She led the way into the sitting room. Then they all

sat by the fire drinking tea while Mrs. Dalrymple told the story of the visit to the hospital, tactfully omitting Mickey's dash to his friend's bedside.

"It was very strange," she said. "He wouldn't speak, but I know he was shamming. I'm surprised the nurses and doctors don't know. It was quite obvious to me."

"But," said Mrs. Trent hesitantly, "what would he want to do a thing like that for?"

"I don't know," said Mrs. Dalrymple. "I'm guessing it's something to do with the shock, but it's certainly not straightforward loss of memory."

Mickey said nothing, but he listened carefully to every word. He was relieved that no mention was made of his own escapade. The meeting was still painfully fresh in his mind, the whispered words, especially that strange sound that could scarcely be identified as a word at all.

Ormingat.

What did it mean?

What did any of it mean?

Mickey watched Mrs. Dalrymple as she spoke, and saw, young though he was, the same look of determination Dr. Ramsay had seen. She was certainly not like his mother. She would get things done!

And if she fixed it so Thomas would be in Belthorp for Christmas, was that really the right thing to do? If Thomas didn't want to come, surely he shouldn't be made to?

The word *Ormingat* shot into his mind again. He shivered. And his shivers, as usual, led to a sneeze. For once his mother looked almost pleased to hear it.

207

"Well, there's one thing for sure," she said. "Our Mickey won't be able to go with you tomorrow. If I'm not mistaken, that's the start of a cold again. He's never rid of them this weather."

"I wouldn't have asked him," said Mrs. Dalrymple warmly. "Two days trashing back and forth would be too much. I'm not relishing the thought of it myself. I'll have to get home now and do some phoning around. Though goodness knows who I'll find at this time. Still, there's tomorrow morning and I do have some very helpful friends."

As the two women went on talking, Mickey went to his desk, took out a Christmas card from the box he had there, and began painstakingly to write.

"Can you give this to Thomas if you see him?" he said, handing the sealed envelope to Mrs. Dalrymple. "It's a Christmas card."

Stella smiled at Mickey. "You can give it to him yourself. Thomas will be back here for Christmas, or my name's not Stella Dalrymple."

"He might not want to come," said Mickey. "He might want to wait there for his dad. You can't make him come."

Mrs. Trent looked vexed with her son for being so forward.

Stella wondered what to say. It was clear to her that Mickey had some childish belief that Patrick would just appear from nowhere, safe and unharmed. She herself had the most dreadful feeling that that would never happen.

"His father can come here for him," she said. "It is the thing he would most probably do."

"But will you give Thomas the card?" Mickey persisted.

Stella took it and smiled across at Mrs. Trent.

"Anything to oblige," she said, slipping it into her handbag.

"He's tired," said his mother apologetically. "I'll be packing him off to bed with some hot lemon shortly. The hot water bottle's in already."

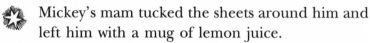 Mickey's mam tucked the sheets around him and left him with a mug of lemon juice.

"I'll be up in ten minutes to put your light out," she said. "Don't forget to say your prayers."

That was what she always said. From his earliest years Mickey had said his prayers all tucked up in bed. Kneeling on the floor to pray was much too dangerous in a drafty house! That would just be asking for trouble, now wouldn't it?

At the end of his petitions, in which he had been taught to ask a blessing on aunts and uncles and distant cousins, he added, "And please, God, bless Thomas and find his dad for him."

It never occurred to him to ask for his own dad to return. But then, he had his mam, didn't he? Thomas didn't. You couldn't count Mrs. Dalrymple. That wasn't the same at all.

Chapter 33

Christmas Eve

Dr. Ramsay was not happy about the arrangement but all morning he had been bombarded with telephone calls and even a visit, a long visit, from two insistent social workers. It was just as the doctor had suspected: Mrs. Dalrymple was the sort who would not take no for an answer.

"I promise you that Thomas will be very well cared for," she said on her third call, when it was clear that the battle had been won. "I know you have his welfare at heart, but I do assure you there is nothing to worry about. Thomas will be back in the hospital on Monday, safe and sound. By then he may even have regained his memory."

Dr. Ramsay knew, and Stella herself suspected, that it was not a simple case of amnesia, but he did not contradict her.

"There are conditions," he said. "You do realize that."

* * *

"Well, Thomas," said Stella that afternoon, "I have come to take you home for Christmas. We'll have to be back here again next Monday, but you'll have Christmas day and the whole weekend in Belthorp with me and Mickey and all of your friends."

Dr. Ramsay had followed her down the ward, anxious to see the boy's reaction to this suggestion. It was, he knew, impossible to predict what it would be.

Thomas looked at Stella wildly. He had been taken too much by surprise to attempt his former impassive stare. But his choice was already made: Vateelin, not Stella; Ormingat, not Earth; Tonitheen, not Thomas. Now he felt trapped.

Stella bent forward and touched his shoulder.

"Get up and get ready to go," she said. He was already dressed in his day clothes. It would be simple enough to slip off the bed, retrieve his jacket from the locker, and leave that ward hand in hand with Stella. It was difficult to know what to say or do.

"Come on, Thomas," said Stella urgently, willing him to make a move.

Dr. Ramsay hovered behind her, ready to remind her that the condition of Thomas's leaving was that he should go voluntarily, acknowledging Mrs. Dalrymple as someone he knew or at the very least someone to whose tutelage he would have no objection. Any sign of reluctance would be enough to cancel the whole enterprise.

"Thomas, Thomas," said Stella in a low and anxious voice.

"I think he is not ready to leave yet," said Dr. Ramsay, quite smoothly but with an undeniable firmness in his tone.

"Give us time," said Stella, looking round at him impatiently. "Just leave us for a while."

Dr. Ramsay was irritated but he withdrew a little.

Stella was wishing at that moment that she had been able to bring Mickey along after all.

"This is your last chance, Thomas," said Stella quietly, grasping his hand. "If you don't come with me now, you'll be stuck here for Christmas day. I won't even be able to come and see you. There's no transport. I know you have problems and I promise you I won't ask any questions. We'll just have a nice Christmas together and that'll give time for other things to happen."

She was deliberately vague, but Thomas knew what she meant. He felt like saying what he instinctively knew: *Nothing will happen if I go to Belthorp. The spaceship leaves Earth at midnight on the twenty-sixth. If contact is made before then it will be with this hospital here. It is from here that my voice was broadcast. Two more days, three more nights. Till time runs out, I must stay here and wait.*

That was the best logic he could manage if he was not to give up hope altogether.

I wish, oh, I wish I could tell you, he said to Stella in thought, words he dared not utter out loud. *I love you, almost as my mother I love you, but you must go away and leave me here. It is my father I need. And my father needs me.*

"Thomas," said Stella anxiously. "Are you listening to me?"

The tug of her voice was unendurable. It would have been such a relief to sob and be comforted, but that would be too perilous by far. *I can't, I mustn't . . . I mustn't, I mustn't, I can't, can't, can't.*

He clenched his fists and his whole body went rigid as if in a fit.

"Vateelin! Vateelin! Vateelin!" he shrieked, looking in vain for rescue from a situation he simply did not know how to cope with.

Dr. Ramsay rushed forward and took Mrs. Dalrymple by the shoulders.

"You will have to leave now, madam," he said. "Even you must see that."

Stella turned sharply and shrugged the doctor's hands away. She was shocked at the voice she had just heard.

"When did you say the psychiatrist would see him?" she said.

"Next Tuesday," said Dr. Ramsay.

"Do you not think it is more urgent than that?"

Stella perceived that they had already heard this voice, that they already knew that Thomas was much, much more ill than she had been told.

"I will be back here on Monday," she said. "And in the meantime, I shall phone every day. I expect truthful answers."

An hour later Dr. Ramsay was outraged to see Mrs. Dalrymple walking along the corridor yet again.

"I thought we had agreed!" he said, standing in front of her as if to bar her way.

Stella thrust a Christmas bag toward him with two parcels in it, one flat, one bulky, both too tall for the bag.

"They're for Thomas," she said coldly. "It was the best I could do at such short notice. I would like him to have them tomorrow morning."

Then, with a sudden afterthought, she reached in her bag, drew out Mickey's card, and dropped it in between the two packages.

Only five children were left in the ward for Christmas, two in the cots in the corner, the other three parted from one another by empty beds and stretches of floor space.

Thomas was one of them. He had slept for no more than an hour. Now he was wakeful. His eyes rested on the silent scene. At the desk, a nurse he had not seen before was busy writing. A lamp shone down on her papers.

Cornelia was the nurse's aide on duty that night. She smiled at each child as she passed by, the smile of someone who knows a nice secret.

Thomas lay back guiltily thinking of how much he had hurt his beloved Stella. It had been a dreadful thing to do, however necessary. The thought of it gave him a weight of sorrow that sat on his chest like a physical burden.

When, oh, when would Vateelin come and make it right?

Suddenly all of the lights on the ward dipped low. The light on the desk was extinguished.

Thomas clenched his fists and waited anxiously for what would happen next, as if his father could appear like the genie in a pantomime. He knew, of course, that pantomimes weren't for real, but they had to get their inspiration *somewhere.* In a world where everything had become uncertain, anything was possible.

Then, in the darkness, came the sound of music. A group of young people trooped into the ward carrying old-fashioned lanterns and wearing old-fashioned clothes. Their lamps swayed and glowed. They walked round ceremoniously, then stood still in the middle of the floor and went on singing.

"O little town of Bethlehem,
How still we see thee lie;
Above thy deep and dreamless sleep,
The silent stars go by. . . ."

This was followed by shepherds watching their sheep by night and finally the rocking carol. All five children enjoyed it; even the youngest stood up in their cots. Thomas too loved the tableau; in some strange way it released his sorrow, and tears flowed down his cheeks. He shrank back in his dark corner and was sorry when the music stopped.

"Sleepytime now," said Cornelia after the choir left

to go to another ward and the lighting was restored to normal. She settled the younger children first. Coming to Thomas last, she found him fast asleep, his face tear-stained. Carefully she removed his extra pillows and eased him down under the sheet.

"Good night, Thomas," she whispered. "Tomorrow is another day."

Chapter 34

The Broadcast
and After

The screen glowed green and swirled and quivered after hours of inertia.

Vateelin had sat with his head in his hands, not knowing what to do next. The machine had closed down on him, not answering his latest call for help. By now he was back into the logic of it. It might talk like a sentient being, but it was only a machine, and if it had nothing to say, it would say nothing.

Now there was clearly something to say, something of some importance, to judge by the strength of the transmission.

The green screen cleared and brightened, then became an image, a real picture. There was Thomas, Tonitheen, sitting in a child's chair shouting out his name, the name of his father, and the name of the planet Ormingat.

Then the screen abruptly returned to its former green glow.

"You've found him," said Vateelin joyfully. "Now all we have to do is go and fetch him. With the power of Ormingat, that should not be difficult. Just tell me what to do and I will do it."

"Permission has not yet been received," said the machine, and then the screen blacked out again.

Vateelin, in anger and frustration, pulled the switch back and forward, in and out of the loop. He too had acquired human traits and could abandon the cool of Ormingat.

"Answer me," he shouted at the screen. "You have no right to stay silent."

The screen glowed again with a dangerous-looking purple spot right in its center.

"You are requested not to violate the mechanism," said the voice.

"Help," said Vateelin, not in desperation but in anger. "Help, help, *help!*"

"You are requested not to violate the mechanism," said the voice. "Such violations impede action."

The screen blacked out again.

Vateelin sat back and did no more. Had the machine threatened punishment, it would have had no effect on him. He knew in any case that punishment was not the way of Ormingat. But "impede action" could be important. The action should be to find a way to save his son. That was an action nothing should impede.

The silence in the ship continued for two long days and nights. His watch told him when it was Tuesday, then Wednesday. From time to time he carefully moved the switch to Off and then back to On again, thinking this might arouse the machine and persuade it to speak. A foolish thought, perhaps, but despair is a breeding ground for superstition.

"Help," he said each time he moved the switch.

But nothing happened.

On the floor beneath, the stellar clock still ticked away, telling not time but time remaining. The globule for Thursday was almost in line. Friday's globule trailed just a little behind it. Only the fateful Saturday's globule, which would complete the trigger, wavered out of sync. At one point Vateelin had a mind to stoop and break the glass and capture it. But common sense told him that this powerful mechanism would not be so easily foiled.

So what was he to do?

Wait.

Pray a little, perhaps.

Despair a little.

And wait.

Then, just as Vateelin had drifted into an uneasy sleep and was dreaming of Belthorp and Jackson's barn going up in flames with children playing snowballs all around it, a voice cried out, "Vateelin! Vateelin! Vateelin!"

Vateelin gazed eagerly at the screen, which now glowed brightly. No picture there, no second sighting of his son. But it was clearly Tonitheen's voice that had come through.

"He's waiting," said Vateelin, "and he's frightened. You can hear it in his voice. Take me to him now or let me leave this ship."

219

"Permission has not yet been received. Directions are needed."

The stellar clock lacked only three globules, and of these one was very nearly in line.

"Stop the clock," cried Vateelin. "Abort the count-down."

The machine did not answer him. It was not geared to explain a second time the impossibility of override.

A few hours later Vateelin saw another globule join the line. Only two left; so little time to go.

In the world outside it was Christmas day. Soon children all over England would be waking up and looking to see what Santa had brought them. And Thomas, in Casselton General, would be one of them.

If he were left alone on Earth, thought Vateelin, *would it be so very terrible? Surely he will go to Stella, and Stella will care for him. Small comfort for his father, but better than none. My son will be left here on Earth but he will not be all alone.*

Then he thought of Walgate Hill and poor Canty. He contemplated the spread of evil, disease, and poverty over Earth. This was not a world he wished his son to grow up in. Ormingat was, in every meaning of the word, a much, much fairer place. To leave Tonitheen here forever was cause to weep.

In the gloom of the ship, there was no distinction between night and day. Vateelin ate food from the ship's larder, a healthy if somewhat Spartan Christmas dinner. He caught up on neglected duties, filing

220

all of the information from his document case into a cabinet contained behind a panel in the wall.

That all the while his heart was breaking made the effort the more valorous. If only the ship would release him, he too would choose to stay on Earth no matter what complications might arise. Nothing could be worse than losing his son. His son and Keldu's.

At one stage he thought, *I am a prisoner here.*

"You have deprived me of my will," he said to the screen, expecting no response. "That is not the way of Ormingat."

And, to his surprise, the machine flickered into life and seemed to answer him.

"The way of Ormingat is to protect."

No more was said, and Vateelin concluded that the phrase he had uttered was yet another key word provoking an automated response.

The slow hours crept to midnight, the start of the final day. The penultimate globule lined up obediently and nine lights in formation swung over the face of the stellar clock like a rod. Only one remained to join the line. It traveled alone in an odd orbit, swinging over the pole as its fellows waved their wand in unison across the clock's equator.

Then, once more, the screen began to glow.

"Prepare for takeoff," said the voice. "You will be leaving the ship for a short time. Put on your outer garment. There will not be much time."

In a daze, Vateelin picked up the sheepskin coat,

leaving the empty document case on the seat beside him.

"You have received permission?" he said to the screen.

"Now fasten both sets of bands around you," it continued, ignoring the question. "This will be a short trip, an unusual one for this vessel, but achievable."

Vateelin did as he was told, addressing no more questions to the screen, accepting that the instructions must mean that they were going to Casselton. For where else would they go on an unusually short trip?

"Ready?" said the voice.

"Yes," said Vateelin firmly.

Something like a firework flew up out of the earth beside the Scott Monument. A spark crossed the sky and was barely noticed. And within minutes the ship had landed in Casselton, in the grounds of the General Hospital.

"You have one hour," said the voice. "That should be more than enough. The ship must seal and self-protect in the hours before detonation."

The final globule flickered past the wand, still out of sync but growing ever closer. It was the last thing Vateelin observed before he left the ship and grew to human size again.

Chapter 35

Christmas Day

Each bed had a large, white-cuffed red stocking hanging from the bedrail. If Jamie had been an inmate, the ward would have been riotous at six in the morning even if he had still been hauling his drip around. But the five patients left in over Christmas were all ill enough or sad enough to need some encouragement.

At the usual waking hour for Christmas morning (and well beyond) three of them were still sleeping.

Evie was already awake. She was waiting for her mam and dad to come through the doorway. She was convinced that they had stayed in the hospital grounds all night, ready to reenter as soon as the doors were open.

The other one awake was Thomas, but he pretended he was still asleep. He was wrapped up not only in his sheets but in a feeling of total misery. He was waiting for Vateelin, and Vateelin had not come and had given no sign or signal of his coming.

Nurses came and went. The day gradually began in

earnest; the stockings took precedence over bathing and breakfast. That was the established routine for Christmas day. Kirsty was back on duty and twice as cheerful, if that was possible.

"Happy Christmas, Thomas," said Kirsty, coming to his bedside, giving him a hug, and handing him the stocking he had not bothered to reach out for. "There's a special package from your friend Stella. And Jamie's dad brought something for you—you remember Jamie. The rest are all from Santa Claus himself. And if they're not, I'm sure I don't know who sent them!"

Thomas took the gifts automatically and silently, just as he would take his breakfast.

The presents from Stella were not actually in the stocking. They were in a separate bag lying at the foot of the bed. Thomas opened them to find a model of the old Flying Scotsman, and a book about all of the trains in the Railway Museum at York. Ordinarily Thomas, who loved trains, would have been delighted. But his anxiety at being stranded in the hospital ruined whatever appreciation he might have had.

He almost threw Mickey's card away with the wrappings but noticed it just in time. He opened the envelope and read his friend's message, which filled the inside flap. It was written in very small, neat writing.

Hello Thomas—I no you mite not get this card I hope your dad has come for you. I no you told me the truth. *I kept the secret but if you get stuck please come home to Belthorp.*

Your dad will come for you but if he's a long time you mite as well come back here til he comes you cud get on telly again. Your friend for always Happy Xmas from Mickey Trent.

Mickey might not be the world's best speller, but, as usual, what he said made some sense.

Next came Jamie's parcel. The die-cast model of a silver plane would normally have been something to treasure. Thomas fingered it briefly, put it to one side, and opened the Christmas card. A single sheet of paper fell out. Jamie's writing was big, bold, and wobbly. His spelling—surprisingly, perhaps—was nearly perfect.

At the top of the page was a properly printed letter heading:

The Sunflower Retirement Home
Kenton Corner
Casselton

Dear Sammy,

I am writing from home but my mam told me not to put our address on the letter. So if you want to write to me send it care of Mrs. Armstrong at the above address Mrs. Armstrong is my great-granny. She's my dad's gran and she's nearly ninety you would like her. That can be our line of comunication.

I am writing to tell you that I think you are a spaceboy

stuck on Earth by mistake. I think you come from a differ-
ent plannet. I know about you seeing the crash on Walgate
Hill. Is that how you got stuck? I don't know how I can
help you but I will if I can. I know how to smuggle things
because my dad is a customs officer. Just let me know if you
want me to do anything. I am coming to the hospital the
Wednesday after Christmas for a checkup. I'll try to get my
dad to bring me then I could come along and see you if you
are still there. My mam doesn't understand about people
from other planets. Yours faithfully, Jamie Martin.

P.S. Nobody knows what I think but me.

Thomas lay back thinking of his old friend Mickey and
his new friend Jamie. He did not weep, but his heart
filled with tears. Why could he not just be a real Earth
boy? Why could his father not just be an ordinary
Earthling? It would be so lovely to have a great-granny
of his very own like Jamie, and a mother and brothers
and sisters and uncles and aunts. And to have a real
and lasting place here on Earth.

Listlessly he put the presents to one side.

He closed his eyes and, almost as in prayer, whispered softly enough for no one to hear, "Where are
you, Vateelin? Why have you not come for me?"

Evie's family were the first to arrive, heaped up
with parcels and softly singing "Jingle Bells."
The little girl was kissed and cuddled by her mam and

dad and had an extra parcel thrust at her by her older brother, who said gruffly, "That's for you from me."

A few minutes later, the sad little woman who came each day to visit the infant in the corner cot came in with a taller, older friend who might have been her sister.

Danny Joicey, in the next cot, was recovering after a very tricky operation.

"He's doing fine," said Kirsty to the company of Joiceys who came in to visit and made the ward just a little bit too noisy. Rules were relaxed for Christmas day and the ward was empty enough to make it unnecessary to limit the number of visitors per bed.

The older boy in the bed nearest the bathroom had very quiet visitors, a middle-aged couple visiting their only child.

Thomas was the only one who had no visitors at all. It hurt.

He was used to Christmas being very special and very loving. And here he was alone and feeling lost. Other children had relations to spare. He had only ever had his father. And Stella—but Stella wasn't quite a relation, was she? Earthlings were very clear about that.

Thomas lay back watching the others, automatically composing in his head the things he would say about them if he were writing it all down. Habit dies hard. Observing had been part of his life for so long that he saw things other children his age might well have missed.

Kirsty was specially attentive, but Thomas barely

looked at her. His decision not to speak held firm. He picked up the book about the trains at York, began to read it and to examine minutely all of the pictures.

"That's the Mallard," said Kirsty, looking over his shoulder.

Thomas nodded briefly and turned the page as soon as he felt it not too rude to do so.

The day passed slowly. Christmas dinner and tea were dutifully eaten. Because of all the visitors to-ing and fro-ing, no attempt was made to have the children eating at the center table. Each bed became more than ever its own little island.

After tea, there was nothing for Thomas to do but lie back and wait yet again.

This time, though, the waiting took another form, a form more frightening. Thomas found that not only could he pretend amnesia, he could somehow cultivate it. With effort, he made his eyes see nothing, his ears hear nothing. Then the muscles of his body relaxed completely, with final twitches in his arms and legs.

"Thomas," said Kirsty briskly, alarmed at the boy's trancelike appearance. "Thomas."

At her voice Thomas came to life again with a jump, as if he had fallen from a ledge. He looked at the smiling face and, unthinkingly, smiled back.

"That's better," said Kirsty, straightening his sheet and tucking him up neatly. "That is much better. I'm going home now. Hope you've not minded too much your Christmas with us. In years to come, perhaps you'll enjoy the memory.''

The thought of years to come was enough to make him fully aware again of his miserable state. He very deliberately veiled his eyes with indifference, as if it were a third eyelid.

Thomas was relieved when Cornelia came on duty. She was quieter and much more serious than Kirsty. It would not be so hard to lie waiting and thinking all evening and into the night.

The waiting became less hopeful with every hour that passed.

What do I expect? Vateelin to come here and claim me? That wouldn't work. He would be asked all sorts of questions, to which he would not be able to give any proper answers. Will he ring the hospital and leave a message for me? That might be easy. He could send me some instructions about what to do next. That's what I would do if I were Vateelin and he were Tonitheen!

Toward eleven o'clock Thomas fell asleep and dreamed of Stella. It was summer. They were walking in Waylie's Wood, carrying a basket full of picnic food. Vateelin was not there. Vateelin was nowhere in sight. They sat down on a tartan rug and opened their sandwiches and drank cups of coffee from a flask. And Vateelin definitely was not there.

Thomas woke up crying. The one thing he wanted at that moment was to be cuddled by Stella and told that everything would be all right.

Cornelia, attentive as ever, heard the sobbing and came to see what she could do.

"What's wrong, Thomas?" she said. The covers on his bed were all crumpled and his pillows were awry. Cornelia began to straighten them.

"There, there now," she said. "Let me make you comfortable."

She felt his brow and thought that, if not feverish, he was certainly overheated. Hospital beds often feel too hot at night.

"Would you like a cool drink?" she said.

The last time Cornelia had found him sobbing, Thomas had stifled the sobs and just listened to her quietly. This time he made no attempt to hold back his tears. He sobbed openly, reaching up with his arms and clinging to the nurse's aide so that she could not finish straightening the sheet. The day had been so very, very lonely.

"What is it, love?" she said. "What do you want? Shall I fetch the doctor?"

"I want to go home," said Thomas. "I want to go home with Stella."

He gripped Cornelia's hands tightly.

"I'm Thomas Derwent," he said, "and my home is in Belthorp. Mrs. Dalrymple looks after me. Please ask her to come and take me home."

Cornelia wanted very much to go and tell others what was happening, but first she had to soothe and settle her young patient. She gently released her hands from his, laid him back on his pillow, and tucked in his blankets.

"Now, Thomas," she said, "try to go to sleep again. I will tell Dr. Jones, who's on duty tonight, all that you have said. I am sure your Mrs. Dalrymple will come and take you home tomorrow, but it's nearly midnight now. There's nothing we can do till morning. I'll fetch you a glass of barley water. Would you like some ice in it?"

Thomas nodded. The crying had stopped and he was ready to agree to anything. Vateelin had failed him. But Stella was still anxious to take him home. That was better than nothing. Yet it was not something to be happy about. Tonitheen at that moment felt as if he were dying, as if his own Vateelin *mesht* were already dead.

He turned restlessly on his pillow. The night would be long.

Then he found himself uttering words he had no right to remember, in the quietest of voices so that no one in the ward could hear.

"Keldu," he murmured. *"Sha Keldu roon."*

And the spirit of his own mother enfolded him and lulled him to sleep. Yet somehow in dreams, Keldu was Stella, because love is love is love.

Chapter 36

The Feast of Stephen

Patrick stood awhile outside the hospital, studying, watching.

Now, at long last, he was in sight of his objective. All he needed to do was walk through the casualty department (the only outer door open at this time of night), down the corridor to the left, and then along past three side rooms to the children's ward.

Would anyone ask him where he was going at two in the morning on the Feast of Stephen? Would anyone challenge his right to be there?

No.

The power of the spaceship would go with him. It was not, after all, so very great a feat. Science fiction is full of so-called force fields, invisible barriers that protect those inside from harm. Patrick's force field was much simpler. It was nearer to the ancient, but true, cloak of invisibility. He himself underwent no physical change. But illusion, a sort of mammoth sleight of hand, rendered him totally unnoticeable. This was Ormingat science, the magic not of supernatural power but of pure scientific fact. People really can be made to see no more than they are meant to see.

The doors to the emergency and accident department opened automatically as Patrick approached. He went in and the doors slid together again. So the doors at least knew that he was there. The receptionist behind her glass panel was totally unaware of him, though he walked right past her. Patients and their friends or family, sitting in rows in front of a television set, did not even look in his direction. The message on the VDU warned that there was a waiting time of up to three hours.

Patrick walked right across the waiting room and out through the swing doors into the hospital corridor. He passed an orderly pushing an old man in a wheelchair. The orderly was vaguely aware of someone passing by but did not look his way. It was not necessary for Patrick to be invisible. He was *not* invisible. He was simply unobserved.

The nurse at the desk in the children's ward did not observe the late-night visitor. The nurse's aide attending a patient in one of the cots did not observe him.

Thomas was in a deep sleep, dreaming of walking with his father up a snow-clad hill and seeing the field where the barn burned down. They were well wrapped up and cozy together, looking forward to a nice hot dinner on a cold, cold day. There was a lot of laughter in that walk and an overspill of happiness. So when some sound outside the dream brought him back to wakefulness he yearned to stay safely asleep.

Then he became aware of what had disturbed him.

The curtain round his alcove was moving. Cornelia coming to see him again? He closed his eyes and kept his arms still and tucked under the blankets. He did not want to talk about the dreadful decision he had made.

"Thomas," said Patrick quietly, coming close to him and sitting on the edge of his bed. "Thomas."

"Father!" said Thomas, sitting bolt upright. "You've come!"

"I've come, Tonitheen," said Patrick. "Did you not know I would?"

Thomas clung round his father's shoulders, hugging him and sobbing.

"Oh, Vateelin, Vateelin, Vateelin mesht," he cried.

Patrick stroked his son's head and murmured, "There, there. It will be all right. Don't worry, Tonitheen *ban.*"

For a few seconds, or maybe minutes, nothing more was said. Then Thomas remembered his betrayal. "I told them I was Thomas Derwent," he said. "I didn't mean to, but I thought . . ."

"It doesn't matter," said Patrick. "After all, you *are* Thomas Derwent. You have been Thomas Derwent for five years. It will soon be sorted out."

Thomas was bewildered.

"You'll explain to Stella?" he said. "You'll tell the nurses? And everybody?"

"Not quite," said Patrick. "Not in the way you mean. Do you not wonder why no one is here asking me who I am? Do you not wonder how I got in here tonight?"

Thomas gave him a puzzled look. "What about Cornelia?" he said. "She must know you are here."

"No one knows, Thomas Tonitheen," said Patrick, "and no one ever shall know. That is how it has been arranged. I am here in secret."

Thomas gave a worried look at the curtain and whispered, "They'll hear us."

"They won't," said Patrick. "We can leave here together, totally undetected. That is the power of Ormingat."

"But Stella will be coming for me tomorrow to take me home," said Thomas, struggling to make sense of everything. "What will she think?"

"Would you rather go with her, son?" said Patrick softly. "It is a possibility. It can be arranged. I can leave without you, but then we would never meet again, not in this life."

Thomas did not speak and Patrick realized how difficult this was for a child to understand—Earth child, Ormingat child, any child at all.

"I want you to make a free choice," he said. "I want to be completely fair to you. Once I said I would never lead you into harm's way. I have learned what a false and dangerous promise that was. If you come with me, you take all the risks I take. If you come with me, you face a life such as you have never known, and you might even have to face death. I will not pretend to offer you safety. All I can offer is love."

Thomas clasped his hands together. His face was pale and his eyes were black as the night.

"You are my father," he said. "I will go wherever you go. Tell me what to do, Vateelin *mesht.*"

"One thing at a time," said Patrick. "Do you have your own clothes?"

Thomas nodded toward the locker.

"They're in there," he said.

"Well, get dressed quickly and then we'll go."

After Thomas was dressed he straightened the blankets on his bed, wanting somehow to signify a voluntary departure. He was worrying about what the nurses would think and what Stella would believe when they told her he was gone.

Patrick smiled as he watched him. Then on an impulse he removed the sheepskin coat, still with its tattered edge, and laid it across the bed.

"Why?" said Thomas.

"A message," said Patrick. "Better than simply leaving a tidy bed. A message for everyone, but especially for Stella. I don't know how much she'll understand, but she will at least know that you are with me."

Patrick held Thomas's hand; it was safer that way, to make sure that the illusion would cover both of them.

"Where are we going?" said Thomas. "How will we get there?"

"First we leave the hospital," said his father. "After that, you'll see."

As they walked along the corridor they passed a glass door that looked out onto a shrubbery. Snow was beginning to fall.

"You'll be cold," said Thomas with some concern.

Patrick, his sweater long gone and his coat left behind him, was now in shirtsleeves. He *was* cold and they were not even outside yet.

"It won't be for long," he said.

They walked out through the waiting room, where the late-night patients were still waiting and the late-night television was giving them news from all around the world.

The outer doors opened and Patrick and Thomas found themselves walking into the grounds through a layer of snow, their shoes and trainers leaving distinctive footprints. Page and monarch forth they went!

Chapter 37

The Last Chapter

They were on the edge of the drive that swept down from the hospital gates to the emergency and accident entrance. Before they could cross, an ambulance came down out of the darkness, its headlights illuminating the fall of snowflakes.

Thomas blinked.

Patrick brought them both to a sharp halt, holding his son's hand tighter.

"We are unnoticeable," he said, "but we aren't indestructible. One accident is quite enough!"

When the ambulance had passed, Patrick continued, leading Thomas across to the car park. It was a tarmacked area surrounded by a dwarf shrubbery. Snow was fast covering everything. The flakes were coming down thicker and faster.

"Not long now," said Patrick, gritting his teeth against the cold as the snow soaked his shirt. Thomas was better-clad but still distressed by the inclement weather. He clung to his father's hand and worried that Patrick would "catch his death of cold," a phrase he had heard Stella use many and many a time.

Patrick looked down at his son anxiously, misinterpreting the serious expression on his face.

"You are quite sure you want to come?" he said through shivers.

Thomas nodded but did not speak.

"I don't own you," said Patrick, remembering an earlier, foolish conversation. "I should never, ever have said that I did. You do honestly have a choice, even now."

"I've chosen," said Thomas clearly, sounding quite grown-up.

Then he added, childlike, hesitant, "What will we *be* in Ormingat?"

Patrick smiled down at him, taking a second to realize what he meant.

"Recognizable," he said with a laugh. "Different, but recognizable. There is no form under which we would not know each other."

"But different?" said Thomas, thinking of all the comics he had read, all of the alien characters he had seen in programs on the television. To turn into a six-legged lizard with crumpled skin and curling fangs was not a pleasant prospect!

"Not completely different," said his father, remembering the monsters in the film he himself had seen just days before. "Not grotesque."

They had come to the far edge of the car park, nearly to the outer gate.

"Are you ready?" said Patrick. "Very soon we will be going into the spaceship and setting out on our course for home. We will diminish. And for a while it will feel very strange."

"Where is it?" said Thomas.

"Over there, to the right of the gate."

Patrick pointed, and in the gloom Thomas could see a bluish glow that, as they drew nearer, he identified as the facet of a crystal. The snow around it reflected a bluish light. The ship itself gleamed like a sapphire, but with an aura of rosiness that promised warmth. This, then, was the thing he had long thought of as dimpled like a golf ball.

"It's more beautiful," he said, and Patrick knew at once what he meant.

"And much more useful, Tonitheen."

The look Thomas gave his father was one of total confidence. Suddenly this was a wonderful adventure just about to begin.

"What do *you* know about them, Mrs. Dalrymple?" asked the reporter, following up the story of the disappearing Derwents and the mysterious coat left draped across the hospital bed.

The coat had been matched with the torn strip. That no one had seen the man or the boy was a mystery still being investigated, explanations unsuccessfully sought. There had been a false trail leading to Scotland, but the Patrick Derwent who had used his credit card there proved to be someone completely different, with an address in Birmingham. In cases like this, as Inspector Galway was beginning to realize, false trails are only too numerous. Incredible coincidences are rife.

Shaun Trevelyan, half-fledged reporter on a London newspaper, thrived on false trails and incredible coincidences. To come to the village and question the neighbors was just the latest of many angles he was trying, a way perhaps of unearthing something the police had missed. Or at least finding a human-interest story, fleshing out the facts, arousing the intimate, personal concern of a million readers.

"They were my neighbors for five years," said Stella, holding her front door not too far open. She was not about to invite this inquisitive young man across the threshold. "I was very fond of them."

"But you can shed no light on the mystery?"

Stella smiled.

"Starlight, perhaps," she said, "nothing more."

Before the reporter could question this cryptic remark, Stella gently closed the door on him, leaving him standing out in the snow.

About the Author

Sylvia Waugh's first book, *The Mennyms,* was published in England in 1993 and was an immediate success with reviewers and teachers. It won the *Guardian* Children's Fiction Prize and was shortlisted for England's highest literary award for children's and young adult books, the Carnegie Medal. Her other books include *Mennyms into the Wilderness* and *Mennyms Alive.* A retired teacher, Sylvia Waugh lives in the north of England with her three grown-up children.